THE HEART AND SOUL OF RAGNAR THE RED

An Immortals of the Apocalypse Prequel

DANIEL DE LORNE

To Shona, Claire, Michelle and Lana
For being the best crew a writer could hope for

❅   I   ❅

Sweden, 1686

A THOUSAND MEN COULD NOT HAVE DONE WHAT RAGNAR and twenty on horseback had achieved. Loaded down with tax collections liberated from the King's soldiers, they plunged into the protection of the forest. A late autumn wind blew at their backs, aiding their flight and bringing warning of any pursuit. Its chill cut through the back of Ragnar's coat.

A thousand men...

He had only to keep a handful of that number happy through the long nights of the approaching winter, and with the day's plunder surely none would turn deserter. One man was no longer his concern; a musket shot ending his life. Ragnar had taken his vengeance and routed the soldiers, lain waste to their lives for killing that one underling, and only stopped when his band demanded they return to camp. He had not appreciated their censure in the middle of his battle haze, but he had seen their reason and ordered a withdrawal. They sought safety now the deed was done.

While the forest called to his men, a warm and comfortable bed in a fine castle beckoned from his memories. He whipped his horse hard. Åke would admonish him for his rough treatment of the beast, and in turn he would show Åke how rough he could be. Much as the young man liked it.

The day's light faded early, helping to cover their flight. The temperature dropped once enveloped in the shadows of the darkening forest, and their speed slowed so as not to endanger the horses more than necessary. One hoof placed wrong and they'd lose the animal. With what they'd ransacked, they could afford another, but he never liked to lose a good horse if he could help it.

His men held their tongues, fearful of drawing attention to their escape. It wasn't the eye of the law they warded against but the malevolent gaze of the supernatural. Despite the months they'd traversed Halland's forests, learning its sounds, its ways and defenses, many of the men still crossed themselves when crossing its boundaries. They warded against the Skogsrå, the seductive female spirit with the fox's tail who drew men into the shadows with her song and stole their souls.

Ragnar put no stock in their superstitions. They were for peasants. The Skogsrå was nothing more than a creation to explain the loss of foolish men who'd wandered off and lost their way forever. But he relied on his men and was forced to indulge their delusions until the day when he had stolen enough, killed enough, and won enough to become the hero he needed to be. Because heroes were denied nothing. The nobility would welcome his return, hail him their champion, and the revenge he'd finally visit upon those who had wronged him, his father chief among them, would be his. Then this unpleasant low point would be relegated to myth and the ghosts of a forest far from his Småland home.

They reached their camp in the last of the natural light, guided by the flickering campfire he ordered kept small. Åke was waiting for him as he halted. He threw the blond and beguiling young man his reins.

"The raid was a success?"

"Was there any doubt?" He dismounted and walked away from the glint in Åke's eye. "Tend the horses." As if Åke needed to be told.

"As my lord wishes."

Åke's breathy subservience poked the embers in Ragnar's blood, but they had to be smothered. Åke could not become another Absolon, not that he had anywhere near Absolon's skills.

Not with his horses. Not with his cock. Not with his heart.

But Absolon had been a warning and one he was doing his best to heed. His men would only accommodate so much frivolity from him, and with winter fast approaching and their chances to raid curtailed, desertion would be the least of his worries. Two fewer men with whom to share the spoils made an attractive reason to murder—even if that meant killing Ragnar the Red.

The ten men who'd remained at camp saluted him as they hurried to unload the loot from their fellows. He and another man would take it the next day to a secure stronghold deep in the forest, their one hope of keeping it safe until required. It was apportioned equally among them; even he took the same cut though he deserved more. He may be their leader, but his act of goodwill and equality ensured only limited loyalty. Three men knew of the stronghold's location—him among them—so he had relative surety that its contents would not vanish.

Though perhaps he could use the Skogsrå to his advantage and expedite his escape out of this outlaw's existence.

The dampness in the air forced Ragnar to huddle inside his coat, the thrill of the ride and the kill having abated. He sought the closeness of the fire but remained standing to surveil the men. Once the horses were tended and the loot deposited, they gathered around the fire. Wine passed hands and Ragnar sensed a tension: the taut frisson between a successful raid and the loss of a brother.

Ragnar raised his cup. "To Jöns. A good man who gave his life so that we may live. Skål!"

"Skål!" The men charged their cups and drank deep. They refilled their vessels and drank again. Murmured conversation limped in and Jöns' demise was soon swept into tales of the raid. Their voices grew louder, a few laughed raucously, and some cheered for Ragnar. Others failed to meet his eye, but he caught the hard twist to their mouths and the accusing glances that passed between them. A loss was still a loss, even for one such as he.

'Ragnar the Red' they called him, though not purely on account of his dark auburn hair and beard. He had fashioned himself into a legend with a firm hand, a generous spirit to his followers, and tactics that inspired fear in great men. But he needed more than the thirty men beneath his command to recognize him for it. It should not be so difficult.

Their Swedish heritage had plenty of Viking heroes to draw from, even if much time had passed since Erik the Red and Ragnar Loðbrók had plundered lands and claimed them for their people's glory. He could muscle his way into those conquerors' fellowship—even if his father and brother never invited him into theirs.

Men bade him sing and he obliged. Keeping his rich voice low to soften their noise, he transfixed them with a ballad of Svipdagr.

He would have gladly counted himself among the wily champion's hallowed company. One day he would. After all, had he not risen against the odds as second son to a noble family and become a great military strategist?

Never mind that his path had deviated thanks to a brilliant—yet failed—rout during a battle against the Russians. Five hundred men slaughtered, his reputation in tatters, and his rank and honors stripped. Those who'd long resented him had taken the opportunity to make his fall complete. His father, a count of ancient lineage, removed his protection once and for all and would never speak his son's name again. In return, Ragnar would not speak his or his line's until he took his place among Sweden's heroes.

Then his father would know how wrong he had been.

His voice took on a hard edge as Svipdagr's quest to speak with the shade of his dead mother grew darker. Not a man moved as he lost himself in the tale that twisted with his own.

Little more than a year had passed since he'd been forced to make his way alone. Well, not alone.

With Absolon, the farmer turned ferocious berserker. Hair whiter than Åke's, muscles bigger, taller, broader, heart more open, more willing, more generous. Absolon— soldier, protector, lover—survived the failed strategy and deserted rather than stay where Ragnar was not. They'd endured the first winter living like common thieves hiding in the forest until Ragnar had settled on his path to restoration.

He gathered men to him, other former military who had become disillusioned one way or another, a handful of peasants who wanted a life of adventure. Absolon had stayed through it all and would have stayed until the very end if not for the others' growing distrust and the shame they felt it brought their leader that he should be so enamored with another man. It didn't fit the legend.

He'd had to tie Absolon to a wall to get him to stay behind. Then he had been free of him. Nothing else could have kept Absolon from his side—nor Ragnar from his—but a legend did not fall in love until after he'd won, otherwise love made him vulnerable. Love made him weak. And if he were weak, he wasn't strong enough to reach his goal. Then who would know of him? Love was what you got as the reward when all travails were finished; Svipdagr knew that. All heroes knew that.

He knew that.

Ragnar finished his song and the men let out a heavy breath. More than one held back a tear, but his heart was cold, even when they praised him. Their cups were soon back to their mouths, and their throats wet with drink, leaving him to sink into his melancholy.

Where was Absolon now? That question opened an ache in his chest that couldn't be filled with the men's prattling. Ragnar drained his cup, drowned his thoughts, and went in search of Åke.

Poor substitute that he was, Ragnar could nevertheless take his frustrations out on rough, ready Åke. He could take Ragnar's contempt against a tree as he fucked him from behind, so he didn't have to see love in Åke's eyes.

Åke who was not Absolon.

Ragnar picked his way across the forest floor towards the horses. Åke had not joined the others in toasting their fallen comrade. The boy wasn't averse to joining in, but the eyes he'd given Ragnar when he'd returned held the promise of one thing. He would stay among the horses, tending to them until Ragnar came and tended to him.

His horse, Seger, whiffled at him and tossed his head. Ragnar stroked his neck, calmed him, and waited, but Åke did not appear. He walked around the horses, searching for sign of the boy.

"Åke?" He didn't call loudly. Maybe he was back at the fire and had missed him, but surely he would have seen Ragnar leave and followed.

A fox screamed in the moonless night and the sound raised the hairs on the back of his neck. He would not take it as an ill omen. He peered into the darkness made blacker by the firelight at his back and shivered. What he wouldn't give to be back inside four stout walls.

He returned to the fire and his men, counting faces as he went. The three men he stood closest to lifted their heads from their chatter.

"What ails you, Ragnar?"

He ignored Nias and concentrated on counting the men.

Twenty-eight.

Åke wasn't there. Ragnar picked up a torch, plunged it into the fire to catch alight, and returned to the horses. Åke wouldn't have left and if he had, someone would have seen him go. He counted the horses and as far as he could make out none were missing, but he admitted he didn't know exactly how many he had. An oversight on his part. He'd grown reliant on Åke's stewardship, a failing that he would have to rectify once the man returned.

He searched for some clue as to Åke's whereabouts. Perhaps he'd gone for a piss behind a tree and would be back any moment, but as he circled the horses, the torch-light sweeping aside shadows that rushed back in once he passed, the light caught the glint of steel.

He crouched and the torch revealed Åke's dagger. He widened his search in concentric circles from the spot and found, ground halfway into the dirt, the silver medallion Ragnar had given him in a moment of sentimentality. These things Åke would never abandon. Dropped? He measured the distance. Had he run off into the forest? Why?

Fingernails scratched down his spine, and he hurried back to the campfire and the men. Their conversation died to a mumble.

"Are you well, Ragnar?" Nias said.

"Where's Åke?"

Three men snickered.

"Perhaps if Ragnar the Red wasn't so distracted by the pretty young Åke, Jöns would still be alive."

Ragnar struck Nias across his pock-marked face then grabbed him roughly by the shirt front. "I'll take no insults from you." He threw him away. "Åke's missing. All of you fan out and look for him."

"Easy, Ragnar," Malik said. "He'll come back. We all know Åke wouldn't leave you."

This time no one laughed at his expense, but he glowered them into putting down their cups. They drove torches into the fire and staggered off to search, sticking in groups of three or four, their footsteps slow and their heads pitching forward from their necks.

He cursed them silently. *Grown men afraid of the dark.*

But their fear contained some truth. Åke would not leave without reason. He checked the loot, but all was as it should be. He returned to the dropped dagger and the medallion and marched into the forest the way they led.

When he returned hours later, his men were already back and asleep in their blankets. He would have kicked them for their abandonment, but his own efforts had achieved nothing. He looked over them in case Åke had returned, but he had not. His heavy heart grew heavier once he realized there weren't enough bodies present. Perhaps some had continued their search. Perhaps others had left him completely. He checked their plunder again and it had not been touched. He checked their faces again, waking more than a few in his frantic search.

Ove and Børge were missing, two men who knew of the vault far to the north. Could they have taken the opportunity to leave and rob him?

"Fret not, Ragnar." Vígarr yawned and resettled beneath his blanket. "Åke and the others will return in the morning."

He kept his tongue and didn't want to raise more fear than necessary. Their packs were still there, supplies untouched. They could not embark on that journey without provisions and they had not taken horses. If they had set course for the north, he could overtake them.

"But what if they do not?" he said, more to himself than to Vígarr.

"Then the Skogsrå has them and may God have mercy on their souls." Vígarr said it so off-handedly but in the light of the small fire his eyes seemed fixed and dead.

He settled close to the fire, wedged in among his sleeping comrades, with his back up against a tree. He would keep watch for any who returned and would welcome them with open arms. But even this close to the fire, he could not warm the chill encasing his heart. Something had happened to his men, whether desertion or worse, and his dreams sputtered like the crackling embers, casting bright flickers that were snuffed out in the darkness.

DAWN'S ICY TOUCH SHOCKED RAGNAR INTO WAKEFULNESS and he berated himself for falling asleep. The fire had long since burned out and cold had stiffened his bones. He rocked out of his seated position, his ass sore from the hard ground. Aches rippled through his back. He cracked his neck. He dusted himself down, straightened his coat and trousers, and rubbed his face of the last remnants of sleep. "Wake up!" It felt good to speak loud and rough and send the remnants of his nightmare fleeing.

The men stirred and scratched themselves. He counted them. And he counted them again. Excepting Åke, six were missing. His chest hollowed. Had he counted wrong the night before? It wasn't possible. He'd tallied their bodies multiple times. His heart kicked up a notch. More deserters? None would have woken before him—he was a light sleeper—but maybe they had snuck away.

Or never returned.

He grabbed his sword and strode off to check the horses. He knew he'd counted *them* right; when he'd done so, fear had not yet clouded his mind. He'd counted twenty-five, but when he did so again there were eighteen. When had they stolen the horses? How had they not whinnied and bucked and pulled him from his restless slumber? But if Åke were involved, he could imagine it. Seductive, alluring Åke with his horse magic. What was this plot that he'd stumbled upon?

Rage boiled his fear into vapor and he stormed back to the remaining men.

"Get up! Which of you knew of this treachery?" He kicked at a still sleeping Nias.

"What treachery?"

The men scrambled from their beds and hurried out of reach of his rage.

He rounded on them. "Those ungrateful swine, your brethren, they have deserted us. They have taken the horses and intend to rob us of what is rightfully ours."

Nias stood and men gathered behind him. "Can you blame them?"

"So, you think they are right to steal from us? Did you help them?"

"My loyalty is not to be questioned, Ragnar. I stayed. I searched for your little plaything. I returned."

Ragnar punched Nias in the face, and he fell to the ground, his nose wet with blood. "I will not suffer your insolence over who I have in my bed."

"You mean you won't be questioned for your blindness, like over Jöns."

Ragnar would run the blackguard through, but Malik held him back.

"Brothers, this is not the moment to fight," Malik said. "Ragnar, why would they take the horses? They wouldn't risk waking us."

"They would if they had Åke," Nias muttered.

Ragnar rounded on him again, but he was quick to back away.

"The spoils from yesterday are still here," Malik said. "Why go to the trouble of stealing the horses but not the loot?"

"For a quick getaway. They are cowards and thieves and—"

"We are all thieves, Ragnar. Do not count yourself any different."

"Then what do you suggest, Malik?"

"I don't believe they would betray us, but if it would help you rest easy, we should split up. Some should head north to check on the stronghold, the rest stay behind in case they come back."

"And which group will you be putting yourself into?"

Malik put up his hands. "I will stay behind if that is your wish."

"Ah yes, so you can be here when they return and run off with them." Who knew how many hours head start they had?

"You've been stuck in the woods too long, Ragnar. You're seeing shadows where there are none."

Could he risk revealing his treasure's location? What would stop them from killing him when they got there? Loyalty? Ha! But if he went alone, he could not hope to win against the seven he might encounter. He needed these men and their violence in the years ahead if he were to gain enough power and infamy to see his father humbled at his feet. He had to trust them a while longer.

He forced down his rage, his muscles softening as he breathed. "Very well. We ride. Now. All of us." He marched over to his bedding and started to pack. Some moved, others did not.

"We will not go with you." Dómarr stood with four other men. "We are leaving the forest."

Ragnar straightened. The others stopped to watch. "Why?"

"You have failed to protect us. You lost one of our men in the battle yesterday, and the Skogsrå has taken others. We have been warned and it's time we left."

"The Skogsrå? Have you lost your mind? Do you believe in children's stories? What else? The nøkker are plotting against us? I hear no violins."

He didn't hear anything but the blood pounding in his ears.

"There is no plot. We watched Ove walk into the forest to search for Åke at your request. We hurried back to where we saw him last and look, we found his hat. He was taken. We will heed this warning."

Words failed him. Their babbling of horrors roaming the forest trapped them in his throat. Could something have taken them? Nobody moved as they awaited his response. Their fear could not be allowed to triumph. Ove probably dropped the hat in his haste. That explained it. A flick of Ragnar's hand cast away their miasmic terror.

"Take your warning then and your leave, but you will go with nothing but the clothes on your backs."

Dómarr reared up. "We demand our share of what we stole yesterday. We fought alongside you. That is fair."

"Deserters get nothing." He drew his sword and hoped their intimacy with his prowess would be enough to deter them from an attack.

"Easy, Ragnar. We want no argument."

"And neither do I. You have shown the yellow of your souls and there shall be no quarrel over the nothing that you are entitled to." He kept facing the five, but his awareness widened to the rest of his group. "Those of you who remain may travel with me to retrieve their fortunes and after that you will be allowed leave to go as you wish. Those who depart now get nothing and should be thankful I don't take their lives in payment." He turned to them. "What say you?"

Doubtful looks cast between them, but most gathered behind his back. He worried he would be run through by some duplicity, but they did not test him. Three, however, joined the five whose foolish fears forbade them from returning their fealty.

"So be it. I'll allow you to gather your packs."

Dómarr spat at Ragnar's feet. "May the Skogsrå take you, though I doubt you'd know what to do with her."

Ragnar did not rise to the smear and let Dómarr and the others collect their things. They were escorted past the horses to make sure they didn't steal any. Meanwhile, Ragnar ordered the camp dismantled and the remaining fourteen men onto their horses.

Fourteen men. When I once had thirty. When I once had a thousand.

He pushed them north as hard as was safe to do so. The uneven forest floor made their pursuit treacherous, but no one begged to slow their pace. If they did, they would be left behind. Above the forest the sun hid behind a bank of grey clouds that wouldn't lift. The air turned damp and the sky threatened rain that did not fall.

Ragnar kept watch for the traitors' tracks, but however they made their journey to the stronghold, they did not go the same way. He marked off the landmarks as they crossed them, splashing through the river where its path split, passing the tree that looked like a sleeping troll. Again, no sign of them, but that didn't matter. Ove and Børge knew the way and would not get those turncoats lost. Børge had been close to Jöns; could this be retribution for his death? None could blame him for it; Jöns had been unlucky.

He comforted himself with the knowledge that they would not have traveled far or fast while night lay thick, but a lead was still a lead and one he had to close.

Night fell swift and the way became treacherous. Malik rode up beside him and asked to halt and make camp. He would have kept going, but his backside yelped from a day in the saddle, and his energy had flagged. He could not fight all those ingrates single-handedly, and though he hated to allow a greater interval, he saw sense in stopping. Once they reached the stronghold, he'd have a better idea of which way they had absconded with his treasure. Still, he ignored Malik's pleas until he chose to stop. When he did, more than a few men swore thanks to God.

One spot was as good as any to make their camp, and the first to dismount struck a fire to ward off the chill, while others tended to the horses. Men took their horses down for water at a nearby stream. A hand took the reins from Ragnar while he oversaw the operations. No doubt they'd return with stories of the young, handsome Strömkarlen playing them a song on his fiddle. Little did they know they had worse things to worry about in these forests, such as wolves that would think nothing of picking off a man or two in the dark night.

The fire light struggled to permeate the gloom. It blanketed him and made him restless for action. Where were those traitors now? How far ahead had they pushed? How much would they steal? And why would Åke leave him?

Because Åke was not Absolon.

They settled with whatever drink they'd been able to carry, and a slim meal of dried meat. It sat cold in his belly. No one spoke. The crackle of the fire and the smacking of their lips sounded loud in Ragnar's ears. He looked from face to face, Vígarr sullen, Nias angry, Malik anxious—

Anxious for what?

And as Ragnar studied him, Malik turned to look back into the darkness, then back to the fire, then out again. His leg twitched. He tapped his hand on his thigh. Food uneaten. Nobody moved as much as Malik.

"Malik." Ragnar's voice sounded loud in the stillness and turned all heads. "What's the matter?"

His mouth opened and closed. "It's…it's probably nothing, Ragnar."

"Out with it. Whatever your fears are I would have them dealt with so they may not infect your heart any longer."

"It's Tordur." Malik swallowed. "He's not here."

Ragnar cast his gaze around the assembled group. *Thirteen.*

The men grew restless.

"He's probably tending to the horses down by the stream."

"He didn't go down there," Malik said. "I would have seen him. I checked everyone who was with us."

Ragnar stood. "Tordur!"

His voice cut through the crisp forest air and carried the desperate tinny tone of his cry.

Nothing answered.

He called again and received the same response.

"I don't like this, Ragnar. He wouldn't have left on his own. Not without his share."

"He's probably taking a piss. What else could it be?"

"The Skogsrå."

"Stop that nonsense! There is no such thing. The only thing that can take your soul is God, and even He doesn't want yours. Go search for him if you wish, but at this time of night that kind of foolishness can get you killed, and not by some figment of a drunkard's imagination." He roared out the last of it, shutting their mouths.

In that silence the crack of a thick stick breaking under foot shocked them into standing and drawing swords. They faced towards the sound and the nothingness it came from.

Ragnar forced speech past his heart clogging his throat. "You see? That will be him returning now." He called out Tordur's name.

A shadow moved in the gloom, too far out of the fire's light to discern to whom it belonged, and the sound of something large moving through the air caught them. Their eye turned to the moving blackness out and over them, and they tracked it with their eyes as Tordur's body fell from the sky and landed on the fire. Embers exploded into the air, scattering his men as they cried out.

Ragnar watched, silent and numb, as they failed to corral their fear. Instead of running towards whatever had attacked, most ran away. The dark swallowed them, and their pleas for mercy were cut short, one by one.

Ragnar's heart had stopped, his stomach had turned to iron. He stayed by Tordur's burning corpse, his sword-point up. Malik ran back to him. No more screams pierced the night. Had any of his men escaped? Considering the speed with which they'd been dispatched, he found it unlikely.

And they had all died because of his failure. Again.

"Prepare yourself." He and Malik stood back to back. Breath heavy and white in the air, the smell of burning flesh stung in his nose. Heavy footsteps turned his head, and he peered across the fire. The shadows took on shape and detail as their attacker emerged out of the darkness. This was it.

The monster was there.

Yet the closer he got, the more familiar he became until the light revealed their tormentor.

"Absolon?"

It came out barely more than a whisper, but in his heart, he knew it for truth and recoiled. Absolon with his almost-white hair, sharp chin, long and thick arms, his brutish build. His mouth twisted in the sneer that he wore in battle. Hate and malice filled his eyes…

Absolon the Berserker.

There was no doubt who'd killed those men and yet he was unarmed.

Malik roared and charged with sword raised to strike, fear spurning him into recklessness. He leapt over Tordur's funeral pyre, swinging his sword down clumsily and exposing his side to attack. Absolon ducked as he landed, and faster than Ragnar's eye could track, grabbed Malik's sword arm and broke it in his grasp. Malik dropped his weapon with a cry, and Absolon splayed his hand through the ties of Malik's shirt to press his palm against his chest.

Malik twitched, like Absolon had plunged his hand through his ribcage and seized his heart, and within seconds, stopped and died. Absolon dropped his body to the floor.

How had Absolon done that with the barest touch? On the battlefield he had beaten men into unconsciousness with one blow of his fist and hacked his way through a score of men, but this deathly touch filled Ragnar with a palpable dread. He held his sword with both hands as Absolon advanced but sweat slicked his palms and his grip was not as sure as usual.

"Absolon? Why are you doing this?"

Absolon did not answer, but the muscle in his jaw spasmed and his nostrils flared with the air forced through them. He stood on the other side of the fire, his fingers curling into claws and the light illuminating his face's fury. Absolon had come for his revenge.

Ragnar stepped back but he would not run. He had had his reasons for leaving Absolon behind. Good reasons. He had provided food and water. He had left him alive. Surely, he could not hold a grudge. It had been better that way.

But quick as lightning Absolon appeared by his side. Ragnar's heart launched into his throat, which Absolon gripped with a strength he'd never known he had.

I'm going to die, and no one will care.

Absolon's grip tightened. Ragnar dropped his sword and clawed at Absolon's vice-like hold but to no avail. Absolon's sapphire eyes blazed with hate, the only thing illuminating the unconsciousness amassing at the edges of Ragnar's vision. Absolon was going to break his neck. He wanted to say something but couldn't get his words out.

Pressure increased until, with a roar, Absolon threw Ragnar to the ground.

He coughed and spluttered, gathering onto all fours and trying to speak. He looked up at Absolon to beg for—

Absolon smashed a rock into his head.

2

When Ragnar regained consciousness, he found manacles clamped around his wrists and the forest transformed to a stone-walled room. Early morning light eked in through the solitary barred window over the stout wooden door opposite. He sat up quickly, pain shooting from his head to pummel his stomach and he rolled over and vomited up what little he had in his belly. His strength failed him, and he sank down next to his rancid waste.

The chains clinked as he gingerly fumbled around the back of his head and hissed as his fingers came into contact with the dried bloody mess matting his hair. Absolon had got him good. But he hadn't killed him.

That was something.

That was something he could work with.

He breathed again, quelling the nausea, and raised himself into a seated position with his back against the wall, slowly this time. He shuffled back and winced but forced the pain to submit to his will. It was just a bump on the head. He couldn't let it stop him. He had to get out.

The door looked solid enough with no rotten planks to

pry loose, but perhaps the lock could be forced with enough strength. The window was too small for him to slip through even if he could remove the bars. And the dirt ground was too compact to tunnel his way out. He tilted his head back and looked at the ring embedded in the wall above him and the chains connected to it. One metal eye to hold both chains. It appeared to be driven hard into the stone. With enough strength and perhaps something to chisel around it, he could potentially wrench it loose before Absolon came.

Absolon had to come. He wouldn't have brought him there alive if he didn't have further designs. Why did he hunt him down? What torture would Absolon visit upon him? What revenge would he seek? As if the slaughter of thirty men and the decimation of his dreams weren't enough. But no matter what power Absolon had, Ragnar would not capitulate. He would get free or die trying. Whatever small regard he'd had for Absolon in the past, it was all for naught. Absolon would not triumph.

As if his thoughts had been a bell summoning a servant, a key turned in the door's lock with a scrape in the rusted mechanism. Ragnar stood slowly, using the wall to catch himself against, until he was upright. He left his arms hanging loose at his side, ready to strike or block. He relaxed his jaw. Absolon would not find him afraid.

The door opened inwards—unfortunate but not insurmountable—but before Absolon entered a small russet-haired hound rushed through the gap. The dog was the kind farmers used to hunt rabbits and foxes, and it darted towards him. Ragnar readied his legs to kick the animal, but with tail wagging, it stopped at the contents of his stomach and greedily licked it up. Ragnar recoiled, but the dog seemed happy enough, its compact and robust little body bursting with excitement as it wolfed down its meal. Within moments the floor was wet only with the dog's saliva and its soiled muzzle was sniffing at Ragnar's boot.

"Trogen, heel!"

At the commanding tone in Absolon's voice the dog bounded over to the shadow blocking the door and Ragnar's gaze followed.

Absolon stepped inside. Ragnar's body tensed of its own accord. Would the berserker fit come upon Absolon again? He'd had to rescue the young soldier more than once from his madness, but that was when there were Danes to fight or the King's soldiers.

That was when the enemy hadn't been him.

But as Absolon's face came into view, there was none of the previous night's rage. Yet his features looked as if they had been chiseled from stone, hacked of its former and familiar joviality and kindness.

Had he imagined Absolon's power? His hands looked as they ever did, as strong as ever but human nonetheless.

Absolon carried a pewter plate with a hunk of bread in one hand and a bucket of water with the other. The keys protruded from the lock, and Ragnar watched every second of Absolon's approach for an opportunity to escape. Without turning his back, Absolon put the bread and water on the floor at the edge of the chain's reach. He could not grab Absolon, even if he wanted to.

There was also the dog to worry about. Its sweet temperament may vanish at any sudden movement. Its teeth looked sharp.

Absolon looked at Ragnar but said nothing and returned to the door. He was going already? Without a word?

"What is this, Absolon? Why have you brought me here?"

Absolon ignored him and pulled on the handle. The dog scampered out. The light grew dim.

"You coward! The least you could do is give me a reason."

Absolon stiffened, stopped, but stayed at the doorway. "You should know the reason, Ragnar."

For all that he had him at his mercy, no joy shone on Absolon's face at having him thus. His voice weighed heavy with sad resignation. Remorse from his captor? From the killer of his men? There was only one reason why Absolon would have done this, and it was the same one that had haunted him—along with the betrayal in Absolon's eyes— the past seven months.

"I left you alive, didn't I?"

"And haven't I don't the same for you?"

"Yes, but for how long? You slaughtered my men and kidnapped me. Why not kill me with the rest of them?"

"It's not your time yet."

"Oh, you'll torture me awhile then execute me like one of the King's jailers? What do you want? Money? I have a lot and you can have it. I have been busy since—" *Best not to mention it.* "It's hidden in…the forest." *Best not to say exactly where.* "You can have it all. As payment for my life."

Absolon sighed. "I don't want your money."

The dog tilted its head up at its master's labored breath, and Absolon scratched its ears, gently, lovingly. He had always been capable of such tenderness.

Ragnar couldn't let himself get distracted by memories. "Then what?"

"You'll find out soon enough. You have thirty days."

Thirty days? Why so many? Why not now? I could fight now. After thirty days in here…

"I was right to call you coward. You are not the Absolon I knew. The Absolon I knew would not baulk at slaying his enemies, would not hesitate and need to build his resolve."

"My resolve is as strong the walls that will keep you here until your last day arrives." He snapped his fingers and the dog ran out. He closed the door and turned the key. The sound scraped down Ragnar's spine like a bony claw.

What deprivations did Absolon have in store? He didn't hurry to the food though his stomach ached for filling. He had to make use of every moment.

He explored the limit of his tether, at first unsteady on his legs, but he regained confidence. How long would it be before Absolon returned? A day? A week? And what nature of jailer was he? Ragnar would have once believed him to be kind and gentle to some—at least to him—but with the look in his eye and the rage he had exacted on his band, he could not count on the false hope that Absolon was anything like the man he had once known.

The bread and water had been put at the very edge of his reach which measured shy of halfway to the door. He walked this half-circle from one wall to the next, right to left, passing his rations until at the other side sat a second bucket, empty, which he could use for his latrine. Both wooden buckets had rope handles. Apart from a couple of hay bales moldering on the far wall, there was nothing else of note that he could touch or pick up. Whatever else had been kept in there had been taken away to make way for the prisoner.

He walked as far from the wall as the chains allowed, then turned and leaned back to test their strength. Unlike the lock, they were newly cast iron. No rust had yet poisoned them, but he wrenched against the sticking place. All to no avail. He went to the wall and probed where the ring had been embedded in the stone. He scrambled through the grit until his fingers cut and bled but could not loosen its hold. Ignoring the dull throbbing in his head, he gripped one chain and levered himself against the wall with one foot, then two, and heaved with all his strength. It would not budge.

Absolon had built his prison well.

Ragnar paused his attempt and returned to the bucket of water. He sat cross-legged, scooped out a handful, and drank. It was fresh. He took another and another, washing away the acid burn in his throat. His body cried out for wine, but his head assured him water was best. He needed to remain clear of mind to plot his escape, because while his chains may appear immovable, no prison could hold a man forever.

He wiped his wet hands on his dirt-and-blood-stained shirt, then picked up the hunk of bread. Expecting it to be stale, he was surprised to find it had some give. He put it to his nose and inhaled the scent of rye. Fresh! A village must be nearby because Absolon had never shown much aptitude for cooking. But wherever it came from, Ragnar's hunger clawed for it. He broke off chunks and stuffed them in his mouth.

Lost in the pleasure of food, no matter how simple, he forgot where he was or how he had come to be there. His throat bulged with the speed with which he ate, and it was only when he was more than halfway through the small amount he'd been given did he force himself to stop. How quickly had he turned into an animal! He was barely better than that dog.

He stopped chewing.

The dog.

Absolon had always been soft when it came to animals. He'd named this one Trogen—'faithful'—and there had been affection when he'd scratched it ears. Ragnar held up the remains of the bread. There was still enough to entice the animal. If it was eager for sick, it would find bread irresistible.

———

THE DAY STRETCHED LONG. RAGNAR REMAINED ATTENTIVE to any sound that reached his ears and his hand opened and closed around the smooth side of the piece of pewter plate he had bent and broken free from the whole in the time that had passed. Absolon stayed away. The dog barked a few times, hours apart, but its excited yapping was distant.

If he lightened his breathing and listened carefully, he could hear the wind blowing through trees and the intermittent bang of a wooden window shutter left to flap in the breeze. No sound of running water reached his ear so perhaps the farmstead had a well. Wherever he was, he was not in a city nor a town. He was not close to a village. He was stuck in the middle of nowhere with little to draw people's attention. The longer he listened, the more certain he was that Absolon lived alone. Or if there were other souls around, they were also captive.

The only other sound of note was the caw of ravens as they circled overheard, sometimes disturbed by the dog barking after them. He counted thirty cries across the day and struggled to not believe the old superstition that ravens were the ghosts of the murdered.

If they were, then they should cry not for him but Absolon.

Either way, they provided no comfort for Ragnar's soul and only helped to strengthen his resolve to escape.

Night came with no sign of Absolon. Ragnar would not wait any longer. Absolon had given him thirty days and he would not waste one waiting. The small window showed only the palest change in the gloom as the stars appeared, otherwise he existed in darkness and would use it to his advantage.

He stuffed the makeshift weapon into his waistband, probed for the bucket of water, and pulled it back to his spot by the wall. He searched for the other, hurling piss against the opposite wall, and taking the bucket with him like a spider collecting flies.

He picked up the first bucket and smashed it against the wall, the crack of wood satisfyingly loud. His heartbeat ratcheted up with the action he'd taken, driven with the determination to break free. The pieces clattered to the floor at his feet. He paused to let the noise settle then picked up the second bucket and did the same. He listened. If Absolon had heard, he'd made no move towards him, but that could be changed. He felt for the biggest pieces of broken wood, hefted one in his hand, and used the window as his guide to the door.

With a deep inhale, he opened his mouth and shouted for Absolon at the top of his voice. He kept up a string of curses and jibes, calling him coward and ingrate and bastard, calling him unwanted and weak, digging through all the small failings he knew cut Absolon's heart to ribbons and used them to flail his jailer. He stopped, gave the silence enough space to grow, then hurled a hunk of wood at the door. It hit with a thud, too light to believe it were a fist if thought about too closely, but in the moment, it might grab Absolon's notice and he may think he'd gotten free.

He threw another piece and shouted again of how he'd broken his bonds and that if he didn't let him out of there soon, he would kill himself then Absolon would be unable to wreak his revenge. He threw another piece and watched the window.

A glimmer of light appeared. He'd come!

He threw another piece and kept up his yelling while grabbing the remnants of bread and holding them in his hand for the dog to sniff and find.

The light stopped outside the door, a small crack allowing it to penetrate into the room an inch or two. Keys jangled. Ragnar yelled again.

"I'm going to kill you, Absolon, before you kill me."

The lock didn't turn.

"You're a coward, Absolon. You can't even face me like a man!"

The key turned and the door opened a few inches for the dog to run in as an advance guard.

Ragnar lowered his hand and whispered to the dog. Soon its muzzle was at his open palm, its wet tongue slobbering over his hand. Such a good dog. Ragnar grabbed it by the scruff and brought it close to his side, bringing out the crude pewter blade and holding it to the dog's neck. He crouched and waited, the dog's tail wagging. Ragnar's hold stayed firm.

The door opened and a lantern cast Absolon's long shadow into the cell.

"What are you doing?" Absolon's voice was a growl that raised the hair on Ragnar's arms.

"Do not come any closer or I'll cut its throat."

"You wouldn't dare."

He crushed the dog and pushed the blade harder against its windpipe. The dog whimpered. "I would. Now throw me the keys, or I'll cut your dog's head off then nothing in this world will love you."

Absolon's breath labored, his shoulders rose and fell, his chest expanded like bellows. Because of the light, his features remained in shadow but there was no mistaking his fists and the gathering rage.

"You're wasting time, Absolon. Throw me the keys and walk away. Once I'm free, then I'll let it go. Do you understand me? That's an order!"

Absolon's breathing quickened. Ragnar opened his mouth to again demand he be let loose and shout above the heavy beat of his heart in his blood, but Absolon roared and charged him.

He didn't have time to threaten the dog again. He let go and raised the blade in defense, but no sooner had he got it up than Absolon drove him into the wall. He held him there, pinned by his upper arms, his strength nothing short of monstrous, and bellowed into his face. He slammed Ragnar against the wall, knocking the wind out of him and cracking his head on the stone.

Stars twinkled in his eyes as his head lolled back and forth. Absolon was going to crush him. He readied to slam him again. His spine was going to break. He couldn't get the breath to plead for his life, even if it could have infiltrated Absolon's berserker fit. Absolon readied him for another blow.

Here it comes.

The dog's whining and whimpering shut Absolon's mouth and paused his throttling. He dropped Ragnar and ran to the animal, but it fled from his master's hand and out the door as fast as it could run, tail tucked between its legs.

"Trogen?" Absolon called softly and ran after it, leaving the door ajar.

Collapsed in an aching heap on the floor, Ragnar rolled towards the exit, spying the lantern that illuminated his prison and his only way out, but the door may as well have been locked and barred for the impossibility of him being able to use it. Dull pain trundled through his body like a wagon, kicking up sharp stones that made him twitch. He took shallow breaths; it hurt to breathe too deep and too long. He didn't move.

And in the distance, Absolon's voice grew softer as he begged for Trogen's return.

❦   3   ❦

THERE WAS NO GREATER TORTURE THAN AN OPEN PRISON door that could not be walked through. Absolon did not return that night, neither to seal the door nor strike Ragnar for losing him his dog. No sound that Ragnar heard indicated Absolon had returned at all. He did not call out for help. In fact, he barely moved from his position, finding the smallest comfort before exhaustion refused to let him keep watch any longer.

When the next day dawned and Absolon had still not appeared, he called out, but no assistance came. He had been abandoned. But Absolon had to return, didn't he? There were still twenty-nine days until his execution. Absolon wouldn't just leave him there.

Not like I did.

He pushed himself away from the ground and the thought. He cringed from each movement. He peered beneath his shirt at the purple bruises spreading across his chest. Had Absolon broken his ribs? The wound on the back of his head had reopened during the assault and blood had dried around his neck. He scrubbed it off, but it only stained his palms.

He saved his breath and his throat, and leaned against the stone wall, hissing against the dull pressure in his back. Absolon had rattled him as if he weighed nothing more than a child. How was that possible?

He scoffed. How was any of this possible? Absolon had killed thirty men with touch alone, had imprisoned him with a strength beyond comprehension, and no order he gave could make the man stand down. He'd tangled with Absolon often enough in the past that his strength, although worthy, had been surmountable.

Absolon had liked being mounted, that was for sure.

And Ragnar had liked it when Absolon mounted him in return.

That had been part of the problem. He'd liked it too much, and it had been a distraction from his revenge.

As those memories now proved. He had to focus, though that was hard with no food in his belly and his tongue drier than lutefisk. The door was open, but how to get through it? As the day wore on, he tried to break free, not caring for the noise he made, though always wary of any sound or shadow that crossed the doorway.

Meanwhile, the question of Absolon's power kept presenting itself. How had he gotten so strong? How had he become so deadly? What would Ragnar do if similarly blessed?

He could slaughter those generals who had ridiculed him and cast him aside. He could exact vengeance on his father and his brother and make them kneel before him like the cowards they were. He could lead the King's armies and cut a swathe across Europe, decimating the forces of Denmark, Russia, and France, all for the glory of

Sweden. Then none would ever hold sway over him again. He would be Ragnar the Red.

Those fantasies stalked his mind while his weakened body searched for escape, but they were both for naught. For that whole day and the next, Absolon did not return. And without Absolon there was no freedom, let alone new power.

Two days and three nights passed. He forgot his hunger, but his thirst raged, his tongue sticking in his mouth, his throat dry and raspy. He licked the stones clean of whatever dew bloomed on them in the morning, but it wasn't enough. He would die of thirst. He dreamed of water, a crisp, clear river running in the distance, so full he could smell it, but no matter how fast or how far he ran, he never reached it. He heard it so close, but he fell, his leg twisted and caught, before he crested the hill.

He was so close…

A waterfall came out of nowhere and drenched his face. He woke coughing and spluttering from the water that had been thrown over him, cold and icy in the new morning. He swallowed reflexively and gasped from his need.

More!

He wanted more, but fear overrode his thirst, and his vision cleared to reveal Absolon standing in front of him with an empty bucket in his hand.

"I should kill you now and be done with it." Absolon's voice sounded like it tumbled with rocks. His fist closed hard around the bucket's handle. The dog was not by his side.

"We both know you're not going to kill me."

"Don't test me, Ragnar. I have killed plenty of men. Taking your life will not be any harder."

"Then why not do it now? Why wait?"

"Because it's not the right time."

"Oh yes, what are we now? Twenty-seven days from my execution. Has someone put you up to this? Is that why you're waiting? My father perhaps? General Lundgren? Is that what this is about? You're doing this for them, so they'll let you back into the army?"

Absolon shook his head. "You understand so little." He said it so softly it was like he spoke only to himself. "None of them care about you, Ragnar. They didn't then; they don't now. What I do, I do for myself."

"Then at least have enough honor to put me out of my misery."

"You dare to talk to me about honor? You think you know misery?" Absolon laughed but it wasn't the sound Ragnar was used to. *Then* there'd been joy in Absolon's voice. *Then* there'd been life. Now it was full of bitterness and a tone of death. "You tied me up in a dungeon with no means of escape and left me to die."

"Yes, I did tie you up, but I sent someone to free you. And it looks like he reached you."

When he and his band had gone a suitable distance, Ragnar had secretly paid a peasant to free Absolon from his bondage.

"You sent him?" This fact seemed to upset Absolon more than anything else. "You sent the Devil to me? It was you who brought this curse upon my life?"

"What devil? What curse? He was just a peasant, missing a couple of fingers on his left hand, but otherwise no different from any other man."

Absolon's jaw tightened. "It was not he who found me."

Then who had?

What did it matter? Absolon had been freed and sought his revenge.

"If that is so, then it was not I who brought you misfortune, merely God or fate." He tried to say it with strength, but a child's breath could have knocked it over.

Absolon knew the flimsiness of his argument too and glared with an intensity that closed Ragnar's throat.

"It is your weakness that has brought us here, Ragnar. I am just a weapon of justice."

"Blather! At least admit this is all your own doing, and I am to die because of your hurt pride."

"My pride?" Absolon's voice lowered until it rumbled with a growl. "This has nothing to do with my pride, but what you have done to my life."

Ragnar would not keep his voice in check, however. "And what about what you have done to the lives of those men in the forest? You took them all with not a moment's thought, even men who had never done you wrong. What had Malik ever done to you? Or Åke? I tell you he was better with the horses than ever you were."

"If he was as bad with your cock as he was with the horses, you should be grateful I killed him."

Ahhh, old jealousy reared its head. "Åke knew more than you ever did because Åke knew his place."

"And it was not in the cold confines of your heart." Absolon stabbed at the air with his finger. "You shed no tears for his disappearance, no sadness at his possible treachery. He was merely a plaything for you to discard. Like I was."

Only Absolon had not been so easily discarded, and when he went, he took a piece of Ragnar's heart with him. But no matter. It had shriveled. Absolon was his enemy now and all enemies must fall.

"Would that you had stayed discarded and accepted you were unwanted and unneeded."

Absolon rushed towards him until his face was a mere

inch from Ragnar's own. "You needed me then as you needed me at the beginning, only your ambition became my undoing. Now it will be yours as well. Finally, that cold and wicked soul you keep locked inside your body will do some good, and its poison will be my elixir. Mark your remaining days well, Ragnar, because they will be your last."

Absolon vanished out the doorway. The door slammed shut behind him and the lock turned. Ragnar didn't move; Absolon's hate had turned him to marble. His hot breath on his face, the grimace of his vitriol, the rage quivering through his body, all swamped Ragnar's own with terror.

Absolon hated him, truly, utterly, deeply, and there was no end to what evil he could visit upon him.

When the fear drained from his body, he sucked the water from his shirt and realized that Absolon's passion would be his greatest weakness. He sneered at the hurt his former lover so readily displayed, at the pathetic performance of it, but thanked the opportunity it presented.

A berserker's fit and a lover's spite were both made of the same volatility and so could be fashioned to another's designs. If Absolon's head had not been filled with woe over past wrongs, he would not agonize so over killing the one who had done him such injustice. If he were calm, Absolon would have slaughtered him in the forest because death was the only certainty. Instead, he waited and allowed his passions to be stoked.

Absolon didn't want him dead at all. He wanted an apology. Why else keep him alive for another month if not to wring a confession he so obviously and desperately needed? What else could the curse he spoke of be? Ragnar's abandonment had been the curse and now Absolon wanted it lifted.

If it meant freeing himself from these shackles, then

Ragnar could do it, as unheroic as it was. Not that it mattered. Once he was free, no one but he would be left alive to know the tale.

ABSOLON STAYED AWAY UNTIL MIDWAY THROUGH THE NEXT day, bringing with him two buckets—one with water, the other empty—and a loaf of bread. No plate.

Absolon's nose wrinkled from the stench; Ragnar had grown used to the stink of his own body and he'd shit as far from himself as he could. He would not apologize for it and stayed seated with his back against the wall to be the first thing Absolon saw when the door opened.

He placed both buckets at the edge of his reach and held out the loaf of bread. "Here."

Ragnar would not crawl like a dog now that Absolon's had run away, even though his hunger had sharpened, and his thirst had brought him close to delirium. He struggled to his feet, wavered a little as he found his balance, and walked towards his former subordinate. He took the bread out of Absolon's hand, surprised at finding it soft and fresh.

"Thank you."

He couldn't keep the emotion of his gratitude escaping his mouth and turned from the shame of it. He stuck the bread in his mouth to stop anything else coming out. His stomach growled from the smell and he barely chewed before swallowing. Maybe he'd choke on it before Absolon could do his worst.

Absolon slipped from the room and returned with a shovel and another bucket to clean what Ragnar had left behind. Like he was a stabled horse.

"You don't have to do that."

"It's for my comfort, not yours."

Ragnar closed his jaw tight. Absolon never used to speak to him in such a manner. The younger man had been nothing but reverent, thankful for everything that Ragnar had given him, every encouraging word, every firm stroke, every deep ploughing. He could not let it rankle him.

"Thank you all the same."

Absolon stopped and studied him with a quizzical frown. He picked up the bucket and walked towards the door. Of course, he would be suspicious. Ragnar knew enough of himself to know he was not one to show gratitude. But damn, did Absolon mistrust him so much? If so, then he had a long way to go to win him over, and he may not have enough days left to achieve it.

Absolon left the bucket outside and leaned the shovel against the wall opposite. He began to pull the door closed. As the light retreated, it wrenched Ragnar's words from his body.

"I'm sorry, Absolon."

He stopped.

"I'm sorry for what I did to you, and I'm—"

"Say it."

"What?"

Absolon opened the door a little wider. He straightened his spine and broadened his chest. "Say what you did to me, so I know you understand."

"I'm sorry I locked you in that farmhouse and left you behind."

"Wrong answer." His hand tightened on the door.

"I'm sorry I left you for dead," Ragnar blurted. "I'm sorry I didn't come back for you. I wanted to. I did. I never wanted to leave you there in the first place."

Absolon filled the doorway. "No one has ever made you do anything you didn't want to do. You think I don't know that? You think I don't know *you*? Tell me why. I want to hear the truth."

"It was the right thing to do."

"Lies. Try again."

"They wanted you dead, Absolon. It was the best I could do."

He flinched but pressed on. "Your best was not good enough. One word from you and that notion would have flown from their heads. They were all cowards, but then again so are you. Now, again, why did you do it?"

"I don't know what other truth to tell you. They wouldn't have stood for you remaining with us."

"Why?"

"You know why."

"Say it!"

"Because you didn't fit into my plans." His mouth twisted on the words, wrung so forcefully from his heart. "I'm sorry."

Absolon approached. "You don't know the meaning of the word, but you'll learn. When your time comes." Absolon crouched in front of him, well within Ragnar's reach, but the scowl on his face was warning enough to not attack. "I had wondered if the deaths of thirty men would make you see, but you have overseen the deaths of hundreds. I was blind to think it would make a difference to your heart, but you are Ragnar the Heartless."

He was wrong. He held onto Absolon's gaze as the shame in his wary heart grew heavy. His men had wanted Absolon dead, as proof of his commitment to their band. It would have assured his place above them.

Ragnar the Heartless.

But he couldn't go through with it. He had been stuck between following his goals and succumbing to his heart. He had compromised and from then, his authority had never sat easy. He had fought them to leave Absolon alone and alive. He'd paid for his abandoned lover's freedom and had worried whether that peasant had completed his charge. He'd passed more sleepless nights than he could count hoping Absolon were alive.

Absolon didn't understand what he had been through. How could he? He was young, carefree, low born, and knew nothing of the pressures of leadership. He only cared for his own selfish ends, one of which Ragnar had enjoyed many times. But no matter how many nights of passionate rutting they shared, the dawn light still came and shone on all of Ragnar's failures. His ambition did not tolerate distractions, and he would not suffer another.

Ragnar had given the apology Absolon sought, but if he didn't recognize it, that was his own foolishness and Ragnar's boon. Absolon would keep returning until he got it and the more singular his focus became, the more he would become blind to a surprise attack.

He fought Absolon's expectant gaze and relinquished nothing until the force of it drove his captor from his cell with a curse. The door closed and locked, but it would not stay so forever.

RAGNAR CONSIDERED STARVING HIMSELF TO DEATH AND stealing Absolon's victory. There was always something aggravating about a prisoner who went to his death willingly, as if it were their choice all along. Where was the justice in that? He'd hanged a soldier who refused to fight another war—against the Danes, against the Russians, against anyone. He didn't resist when they took him, didn't cry when the noose went around his neck, didn't even ask for a bag over his head, though they'd put one on him anyway. He called them cowards but had died just the same. To that hanged man, death was not punishment but triumph. Ragnar couldn't remember his name, but he'd taken his lesson.

Only death was not an option. He wanted his freedom. And with Absolon's considerable strength and the cursed touch of his hands, there was little hope of besting him in a fistfight. He would have to sneak away. But to do that he had to win Absolon's trust.

Before, he had earned it in his bed, but that now seemed an unlikely option. He had time, limited though it was. He could find a way. All heroes needed some skill at diplomacy, at wringing secrets from their foes, and dripping poison into their ear. He already knew plenty of Absolon's: his need for companionship, his tenderness for weaker things, his trust in those who were his betters.

Only he didn't know who or what Absolon had become. He had to find out. That would be the key to his freedom.

He passed the hours listening to the sounds beyond his cell, using a concentration that started aggressive in its nature, but later softened to a meditation with each noise passing through his awareness. Much of the day was silent. Again, no people. Again, the wind. Again, the caw of ravens. But as for the sounds of farm life, there were none. Whatever Absolon was doing out there, it wasn't much. For someone who craved the love of others, he had chosen a strange abode. It appeared the dog had been his only companion. Where was he? And why did Absolon live such a winnowed existence?

The only conclusion he could reach was that he was hiding.

This was not his true home, merely borrowed. If it were his, he would have filled it with horses and other beasts, but that required a working farmstead to keep them alive. Absolon knew this. He had been born on one but escaped its trappings. He should have been able to grow hay to feed them, so then why hadn't he? Could it be that it would draw the attention of passersby, or the nearest village?

Absolon craved attention, Ragnar's more than most, so what had happened to make him hide out there alone?

Ragnar hadn't yet found a way to break his own chains, but he'd found a chink in Absolon's armor.

Absolon didn't return to him for the rest of the day and there was no sound that indicated he was even around, though he must have been. A jailer never wandered too far from their prison, otherwise what did they become without it?

When night fell and the air grew still and crisp, Ragnar stood and faced the window, getting as close as he could without straining. With face turned to the opening, he opened his mouth and sang.

His rich tenor voice had swayed lovers—women and men—into his arms, and Absolon had stared at him with adoring eyes more often when his mouth was engaged in song. His throat was still scratchy from its parching, but the more he sang, the smoother it became. The stone cell amplified and resonated the sound, pleasing even to his ears. He raised his voice louder, as he sang of love lost.

By the third song, his own heart was aching as he poured as near to true emotion into his words. The glow of a lantern appeared in the window, soft at first before getting nearer. Ragnar smiled but kept singing, and the light stayed. He finished the song and moved on to another; one he'd been saving for this moment. He allowed a moment of silence, to let anticipation fill the break between one and the next before he began.

Ragnar imagined he was singing to Absolon, that the berserker was in front of him, naked in his bed and looking up with admiring eyes. He'd sung this song to him so many times: in a crowded tavern when it had been a secret sign of their affection, or whispered in his tent before the start of that fateful battle, and as a gentle lullaby in that cold stone building in the forest while they fended off winter.

He sang all six verses, leaning heavy on the emotions. They were easy to draw on. The memories swept them into his arms. His voice broke more than once as he tripped over loving remembrances and the good times in the bad that they had shared before he'd had to do what he'd had to do.

He held the last note as long as he could, and when he finished, he was no longer looking at the window, no longer playing for Absolon, and no longer in the mood for singing. He retreated to the wall and slumped to the ground, his heavy heart bringing him even lower. He watched the window for as long as he could stay awake before sleep claimed him.

And the lantern never left.

THOUGH HIS RENDITIONS HAD BROUGHT NO ONE TO HIS rescue, he would try again—only when his heart was not so tender. The singing had affected him more than he would have imagined, stirring up recollections from a lifetime ago.

Absolon came in the afternoon with food and water, tending to him as he would a caged animal. He didn't meet his eyes, merely looked at buckets, at manacles, at pieces disjointed from the whole, and not at the one they were all connected to. Ragnar had never felt more invisible.

Words pricked his tongue, eager to leap forth and ensnare Absolon, but he didn't know which ones to use. He couldn't talk about the singing without it sounding like he wanted his approval. He didn't want to lead him into a fight that could push him away. He'd come two days in a row; breaking that streak could prove deadly.

Though Absolon ignored him, he studied Absolon. He forced himself to not linger on his broad build, on his thick arms and coarse hands, on the expanse of his chest and shoulders, the muscles that rippled beneath his clothes, the firmness of his legs or the solid roundness of his ass. All that was as much as it ever was. Even in his studied avoidance of focusing on them, snatches of memories of running his hand across Absolon's naked body, gripping hard to his wrists and pinning him down with all his strength as he willingly submitted, of his hands at his throat—

Snatches that Ragnar had to dash aside in the hope Absolon didn't see how the crotch of his trousers tightened.

No, what he was meant to be looking at was the effect of the songs, the effect of killing thirty men, the effect of being alone with a man he despised. He focused.

Absolon's smile was gone.

That revelation struck him like Thor's thunderbolt.

Thinking back, he hadn't seen Absolon smile the entire time, but he'd had other things to worry about. Now, however...

Gone with the smile was also the happiness that had once filled Absolon's body to bursting. From what Absolon had once told him of his past, there had been little cause for mirth, yet he had always found something to smile at, such as the gentle greeting of his horses and the grudging affection of others. No matter how many times Absolon was spurned, by family, by friends, by lovers, he held onto the hope that next time would be better.

When had Absolon last smiled?

Absolon's eyes swam in sadness, his body was tensed and rigid, he was barely capable of holding himself together.

"Stop staring at me," Absolon growled and turned his head so their eyes finally met.

"Is that to be a new condition of my captivity? You may as well blindfold me."

"How about I pluck out your eyes instead?"

You wouldn't. He tried to believe that.

"What happened to you, Absolon?"

"You dare ask me that?"

"I do. I want to know."

"You no longer have the right."

"It can't be easy for you here, with no one to talk to."

"Who says I'm alone?"

"Oh? There is someone else here, after all? Another jailer? Another prisoner?"

The corner of Absolon's mouth twitched.

Ragnar waved away the need for him to answer, taking the pleasure of having Absolon flustered into his heart, though it didn't ring with as much joy as he expected. "It doesn't matter. I've been listening. I know you're here alone. That must be difficult for you."

"I don't need anyone."

"Come now, we know each other better than that. That's why you had the dog."

Absolon's eyes flared.

Ragnar ducked his head. "I am sorry about that. I didn't mean for it to run away."

"*His* name was Trogen."

"Sorry, again. I was only trying to escape; you can't blame me for that."

"I blame you for a lot of things, including the loss of my dog."

"He'll return. I'm certain of it. You take good care of your animals."

Absolon looked over his shoulder, perhaps thinking of the dog and wondering where it was, and if he should go look for it.

"Who brought you here, Absolon?"

He spun round. "No one. This is my place. It's for me and me alone."

"Has it always been just you?"

"Yes."

"Then where did you learn how to…you know…?" He put up a hand, slightly bent the end of his fingers, and opened his mouth like he was a monster or attacking wolf.

"That's none of your business."

"I think it is." He stood. "It's how you're going to kill me, isn't it? How does it work?"

"I'm not talking to you about it."

"What happens when you do it?"

"You'll find out soon enough."

"But I want to know now."

"All you need to know is that you will get what you deserve."

"Whatever has happened to you has obviously made you stronger and more fearful. Isn't that enough?"

"You might like being feared but I don't. Because of you, I have been turned into this…thing. I am cursed and it is because of you."

"Who cursed you?"

"Someone else I was wrong to trust."

"Then they should be here in my place. I did not do

this to you."

"If you hadn't left me behind, then he wouldn't have found me. I wouldn't be like this. I would have been beside you and we would—" He stuffed his words back down his throat, closed his mouth, and breathed deep through his nose. "What's done is done and you will pay the price for your part in it." Absolon headed for the door.

"Then let me pay for it with money. I promise you can have all of it. Use it to buy yourself a whole herd of horses and a pack of hounds. There's enough there to keep you and your farmstead for fifty years."

"Fifty years? And what of beyond that? What will become of me then?" Absolon grew agitated from the idea and fidgeted and fretted like he was the one trapped in a cell. Ragnar had exaggerated the depth of his coffers, but surely Absolon did not believe he would live much beyond his seventieth year. Very few farmers ever did. But it seemed a question that bothered him immensely.

"There will be someone for you, Absolon. Someone who treats you the way you deserve to be treated. Someone who loves you."

The words shook as they came out of Ragnar's mouth, but they stiffened Absolon to stone and his gaze narrowed. The agitation fled.

"Your money is worthless, and your attempts at bargaining are clumsy and insulting. You will die, Ragnar. And that is the end of it. Hold your tongue and keep your own counsel until then, and pray God forgives you because I sure as Hell won't." He slammed the door.

That night, Ragnar sang again, his breath clouding as it left his body. The glow of the lantern appeared, but Absolon did not demand he keep silent. And though the songs remained melancholy, Ragnar's heart filled with hope.

$$\maltese \quad 4 \quad \maltese$$

Absolon delivered the next day's rations without engaging in anything remotely resembling conversation. No shadows darkened his eyes but the stooping of his shoulders, the lank fall of his blond hair, revealed more about his state of mind than any words. Absolon had always been obvious. No matter how much Ragnar goaded him into talking, peppered with gentle and caring questions about his wellbeing, Absolon completed his tasks like a ghost locked in the work of a doomed eternity.

Old buckets taken out, new buckets brought in, loaf of bread delivered, staler than the day before and dotted with holes where Absolon's thick fingers had penetrated too deep. With the work done and Absolon about to leave, Ragnar ordered him to stop.

And he did, but the set of his jaw showed how much he hated that he had.

The soldier was still in there. How many times had he barked orders at Absolon only to have them eagerly completed? How many times had he spoken quiet but hard in his ear for him to roll over, to raise his hips, to touch himself, to not touch himself?

"Thank you for what you have brought me, and I know you are trying to make this as comfortable as you'll allow, but it has been a few days and I would like to bathe. Even horses get groomed daily."

"You are not a horse."

"Exactly. I am a man."

Absolon chuckled. "You are a viper and spit only venom."

"That may be the same, but the stench coming off me must be worse than any poison. Bring me a change of clothes and a few extra buckets of water so I may wash."

Absolon's mouth twitched. "You think you can make these demands?"

"They're requests. You're in charge. I know that."

He narrowed his eyes. Those words would have sounded false to anyone, but it was nevertheless what Absolon wanted to hear. He was in his power, but though he suspected a trap, he'd consider himself strong enough to outplay it.

"Please, Absolon, I know I will die for what I did to you and the pain I have caused you. I am prepared to wait, but surely you can permit this small allowance."

He grunted by way of response, committal neither one way or the other, and left. If he didn't return, Ragnar would keep at him until he relented. Or made a mistake. The idea of washing had not been one he had planned on, desperate for anything to keep Absolon talking, to find where the boundaries stood in what he would permit. But now the idea was out it seemed as good and as useful as any. An opportunity to wring of potential. Could he convince Absolon to remove the manacles? Could he get close enough to steal the keys or to wrestle Absolon to the ground and best him? The last seemed impossible but desperate men were sometimes blessed with untold strength, and he was becoming desperate.

His plotting was interrupted by the unlocking of the door. Absolon's booted foot kicked it open and he marched in with a barrel full of water held on one hand and balanced with the other and advanced towards Ragnar as if he meant to throw all of it at him. Ragnar retreated, his arms up.

"No, no, that's not what I meant. Please, Sol."

Absolon stopped. "What did you call me?"

"I'm sorry, forget it."

"What. Did. You. Call. Me?"

Ragnar swallowed. "Sol."

Absolon growled and dumped the barrel on top of him. A few hundredweight of icy water drenched him and forced him to his knees. The water flooded the floor.

"You don't get to call me that," Absolon snarled. "Ever again."

It was a mistake. He hadn't wanted that far too familiar name to cross his lips. That had been his name for Absolon, the one he'd whispered in the dead of night to soothe his worries. It had felt sacred then and profane now.

Absolon marched for the door.

Ragnar's teeth chattered loudly. "You can't…leave me…like this."

Absolon sneered. "You'll dry."

"I'll die…of…the chill…before…you kill me." And he believed it. His skin grew taut and gooseflesh rose across his body. He hugged himself for some warmth but that squeezed out more water. He was going to die from this.

Absolon grumbled and vanished. Ragnar tried to look

up, but he was shivering too badly. There had been frost on his water ration that morning and his coat was already struggling to keep him warm. One night like this and he'd freeze.

Booted and dry clothed legs appeared in front of him. "Stand up."

He did as he was told, digging deep for his noble dignity, but no sooner had he straightened than Absolon's hands were on him. With both hands he ripped the clothes from Ragnar's body like they were nothing but tree bark. Ragnar started, about to cover himself, but forced himself to stop. He would endure this. He could perhaps even use it. He held his tongue and watched for the right moment, while the gentle wind scoured his body.

Absolon flung the rags down in a sodden heap. Though the cold would not be flattering, Ragnar stood proud in his wet boots and tracked Absolon's eyes wherever they went. They slid down his body, explored where his hands and mouth had once traveled, but they did not linger. Absolon was a stablehand and Ragnar was a horse being checked for burrs and nicks. Absolon's lips disappeared into a thin grim line.

He handed Ragnar a cloth to dry himself, holding it out at arm's length. Ragnar took it, overreaching far enough to touch Absolon's hand. He withdrew like he'd been scalded and retreated to the other side of the cell, cloaking himself in shadows.

"You're going to stand there while I do this?"

"I don't trust you. When you're done, I'll take everything back."

Ragnar shrugged. He was still cold, his skin tightening on his bones, his boots soaked through and freezing, but he took his time and let Absolon take in all of him. He looked into the shadows to where Absolon's eyes must be before letting the cloth cover his face. He rubbed his hair dry for far longer than he needed.

He ran the cloth over his face then lengthened his neck to mop it of water and twisted and reached as much of his back as he could, knowing how his muscles stretched, creating a line for Absolon to follow. He dried one arm, long, languorous, then the other, before wiping down his chest, his abdomen, deviating to his left leg, down his thighs, around to his hamstrings and calves, and repeated it down the right.

He straightened and rubbed the cloth over his groin, cleaning his cock and balls of the last drop of moisture. Despite himself—or because of himself—his cock thickened but he turned his back before Absolon could see his full arousal.

He held the cloth out from his body. "Will you dry the rest of my back, please?"

He heard Absolon move and smiled to himself but no sooner had his lips curved than Absolon pushed him against the wall, hand flat in the middle of his back, and crushed him against the stone. Roughly, Absolon scraped the last of the water from his body, his bulk close enough to his naked skin to feel heat. Absolon's lips appeared close to Ragnar's ear, hot breath on his skin, lulling Ragnar into closing his eyes. Absolon hadn't often been like this but when he had…

His cock hardened even as Absolon pinned him down.

"You always were a cheap whore, Ragnar."

"Then use me, Sol."

Absolon pressed him harder against the wall. "I told you not to call me that." His teeth were clammed shut so tight Ragnar could hear them grind. "You're not worthy of it."

"Then punish me for it. Take out your hate on me. Use me like I used you." He swallowed hard. He'd stop at nothing to get away from Absolon. Even this.

"You're not worth my spit, let alone my seed."

"You used to enjoy giving me both."

Air snorted through his nostrils. "Is there nothing that will stop your mouth?"

"You know the only thing that could ever do that." He pushed his ass back until he rubbed against the hard bulge in Absolon's trousers and raised a small smile to his success.

"Will you give up what scraps of honor you have left to get your way?" Absolon shoved him again and stepped back.

Ragnar rolled his shoulders and turned around. His cock was standing firm and to attention, but he wouldn't hide it. As much as he hated that Absolon had brought this out of him, he would use it to his advantage. "Why shouldn't we both have a little pleasure before I'm to die?"

"You don't deserve it."

"Then what about you? What about what you deserve? After I'm gone, who will be there for you? No doubt you can have any you turn your attention to, man or woman, but who is there alive who knows you like I know you?"

"And what good has that done me?"

"Take pleasure where you can get it, Sol."

He flinched away from the name but didn't rail against it. "Pleasure is not what I want from you."

Absolon's disdain struck flint in Ragnar's heart, and Absolon's mewling cowardice stoked his anger. "Oh yes, you want my life because you think it will make things right, but it won't. Mark my words it will only ruin you. Those deeds will haunt you for the rest of your life. Take it from me."

"What have you ever regretted? Ragnar the Heartless cares for nothing and no one."

As quickly as his ire flared, Absolon's words doused it, leaving behind smoke and ash. "You're wrong, Sol. I do know what it means to have a heart and I know what it means for one to break, and I regret breaking yours."

Absolon looked as if he'd been struck. "The Devil should come to you for lessons in lying. You speak nothing but falsehoods."

"It is the truth."

"You think a stiff cock is proof enough?"

"That's just a bonus."

Absolon sneered.

"I cared for you, Sol. I regret what I did to you. I…I am ashamed of it. Ever since I left you behind, I have thought of you and wondered how you fared. I hoped you had made it out of there and made a better life for your-self, much better than the one I could have given you." He hadn't planned to say all that. And he hadn't planned for it to hurt so much.

"I didn't want another life. I wanted the one we had." Absolon thumped his chest, and pain twisted his features. "Together."

"I know, but it was impossible, and I'm sorry. I'd do anything to make that up to you."

"You will." Abruptly, Absolon left the cell.

Ragnar backed away a little, a small trace of fear at what he would return with, but when he reappeared, he carried in one arm a thick brown woolen blanket and a change of clothes, and a stool in another. He placed the dry clothes on the stool. "Get dressed." He didn't look at Ragnar.

Ragnar had never before felt more naked and exposed and rejected. If he could not offer his body nor his heart, then what could he possibly give to save his life?

Absolon slunk from the cell and locked him in, and in the pale afternoon light, Ragnar dressed and huddled beneath his blanket.

THAT NIGHT RAGNAR SANG FOR HIMSELF AS MUCH AS FOR Absolon. He paced the cell as far as he could, the ground still cold, damp and turning to ice, as the temperature plummeted. Unpredictable autumn eager to become winter. He couldn't get the shirt on over the manacles but wrapped it over his shoulders and cowered beneath the blanket for warmth. The trousers were good enough. If it hadn't been for all that water and the sodden earth, he would have been warmer than on any other night. A shame there was nowhere dry to lie down.

The sad songs of loss only made the night colder, and so he turned his voice to songs of hope and love found. One of which had been a favorite of Absolon's, one that he'd sung only for him, and as it flew from his mouth and fluttered in the rafters, his heart soared with it, forgetting for a while about how and why he was there, and that it was the two of them once more in happier times.

He had been kinder to Absolon then. He had basked in the younger man's idolatry. Surely, he had not always treated him so harshly? There had been tenderness, other-wise why would Absolon have stayed with him? Why would he have abandoned a good life for the rough one they'd traded it for?

Soon after they'd left the army and gone skulking off into the countryside, they'd gotten into trouble in some backwater tavern in a town that stank of pig shit. They'd been hassled, someone had threatened Ragnar, and Absolon had gone into his berserker fit. He'd cracked skulls, broken tables and chairs, terrified the locals and tackled four men at once. But when Ragnar intervened and the cowards had slunk away, Absolon saw him and calmed, the shame crashed over him, thinking he'd done Ragnar wrong. He'd taken Absolon's hand and they'd run from the tavern, and Ragnar had soothed the beast within, and made love with such gentleness yet such ferocity that Absolon had been revived.

At no point during the whole ordeal had Ragnar thought about himself, only about Absolon. And he knew then that Absolon would be his downfall.

If anyone threatened Absolon's life, he would be undone. He was the weak spot that he could not have if he were to seek his revenge. Because if Absolon tried to turn him from it, he would do it.

When that memory flooded him, he stopped singing, and though Absolon's lantern light remained outside his door, he did not sing again. A restless night passed in which the cold in the cell could not rival the chill in his heart.

***

"Your singing is getting better." Absolon brought food and water, this time adding dried fish to the dark rye bread.

Ragnar's mouth watered, and his fingers primed ready to stuff the lot in his mouth once Absolon was gone. "I'm glad you think so. Do you have any requests?"

Absolon's lips twitched as he considered the question, even though Ragnar had meant it as a joke.

"*Hitta mig på morgonen,*" he mumbled.

Ragnar was shocked. "I thought the one about the boy with the horse was your favorite."

"It used to be."

Used to be... Back when we used to mean something to each other.

"I'll remember that. Thank you for the fish."

Absolon grunted. "You haven't put on your shirt."

Ragnar closed the blanket tighter around his shoulders, unwelcome shame sliding through him over the display he'd made of himself the day before. He rattled one of the manacles. "Bit hard to do with these on. I'm fine, though. The blanket is warm."

Absolon removed the keys from the lock and closed the door, shutting them both inside. "Stand up." He held the smallest of the three keys in one hand and his other hand flat.

His heart kicked up its rhythm. He could get out. The keys were so close. He could snatch them from Absolon's grip, throw the blanket over him and strike him across the head with the stool, buying time to unlock the manacles and the door and run.

Only it wouldn't work, and his desire to flee was some-what tempered. Better to be prepared than foolish.

He stood, kept his fists tight beneath the blanket. "What are you doing?"

"I can't have you getting sick."

"I told you I'm fine."

"And I'm telling you you're not. You're covered in gooseflesh and shivers rack your body. Do as you're told for once."

Ragnar smiled benevolently.

"Don't look at me like that. Give me your hand."

He placed his manacled right wrist onto Absolon's waiting palm.

"Don't try anything."

"I wouldn't dream of it." Ragnar's smile broadened.

Absolon grumbled and undid one manacle, watching him the whole time, ready for anything he might do. But he was not about to fuck up this gift. Ruining Absolon's trust now would only put him further from an escape. His need to play fast and get out faster was replaced with a smarter strategy. Absolon had shown how much he cared for and needed him. A whole month together would be more than enough. Hell, with the way Absolon was behaving, he only needed a few more days.

He lifted his arm free of the shackle and held up his other. Absolon monitored him, but seeing no subterfuge, he let the chain drop. It hit the ground with a clang. He unfastened the other manacle.

I'm free. Ragnar rubbed his wrists gently; the skin having worn away close to bleeding. He fought a wince.

"Do they hurt?"

"No, and if they did, it would be no more than I deserve." He shucked off the blanket from around his shoulders, folded and put it on the stool, then pulled the shirt over his body and tied the cords at his neck. The chill and the irritation of coarse wool on his skin abated. "Thank you." He picked up the chains where they'd fallen and held them up for his bondage to be reinstated.

Absolon took up the manacles in a daze, as if he didn't expect such compliance and was rightly wary of a trap, but he bound him just the same.

The irons weighed heavier on Ragnar's wrists, a small protest after feeling so light and free, a sinking regret that perhaps he should have taken his chance. At least then he'd have died a hero, a warrior who had never succumbed to another's will. But heroes of old had always been wily and there would come a time when he could work his way free without needing to rely on luck. He could wait.

Absolon let him go but Ragnar reached out slowly and touched his hand, gentle and tender. Absolon froze.

"What happened to you, Sol?"

Absolon withdrew from his cold caress.

"Who did this to you? Who made you into this?"

"You did." Absolon hurried to the door and stuck the key in the lock.

"If only I had such power. What *really* happened? Let me know the full weight of my sins."

Absolon leant his forehead against the door and sighed, submitting his whole body to it. "What do you think happened to me?"

"If I believed in fairy tales, I'd say some elf found you and granted you a few wishes, making you strong and deadly, and gifting you with the power to seek your revenge."

"And what would I have given for that?"

Ragnar smiled. This was just some game. Absolon could have easily made himself stronger through lifting heavier and heavier things. He could have trained himself to be faster. The way he killed the men, though…surely there was a reasonable explanation. Poison touch? Concealed knife?

But he'd play along.

"Well, usually you have to pay with your soul."

Absolon turned mournful eyes towards him, hard to see in the dim light but clear enough. And the sadness in them gripped Ragnar's throat.

"Absolon, tell me what really happened. I want to know."

"You won't believe me."

"I will. Whatever you tell me, I'll believe you believe it to be true."

"That's not the same thing."

"No, but for your own good—"

"Since when do you care what's good for me?"

"I'm sorry. I see that whatever has happened to you has been a lot to bear. You might say you've not been lonely out here, but I can see it, Sol. This has taken its toll. Give me your burden, otherwise my death will be as insignificant as the deaths of those men."

He screwed his eyes shut. "Those deaths weren't insignificant. Each one hurt." He opened his eyes. "You would be far better suited to this life than me."

"What life? I could not be where you are. My soul is too restless for it."

"And I know that more than most." He turned away. "And I'll know it even more than you when this is over."

"Please, Sol, tell me what happened."

Absolon wrenched the door open and stalked out. Ragnar could hear him out there, marching up and down, his breathing getting heavier and heavier. Another fit was coming to take him but there was nothing for him to attack.

"Absolon! Come back!" He strained against his manacles, getting as close to the door as possible. "Don't let the fit control you. Let me help you."

And he wanted to. He should have welcomed this discomfort and Absolon's decline, especially if it turned into a fight. He might be able to get the keys from him or wring some advantage from the situation, but the sight of Absolon's pain had quelled those desires and stoked another. He wanted to soothe the beast.

"Don't give into it! Come back to me!"

Silence.

Ragnar's blood beat through his arteries.

"Sol?"

Absolon roared and charged into the cell, his hackles were up, his muscles bulging, his eyes wild and menacing. Ragnar swallowed hard and braced as Absolon's whole weight bore down upon him and crushed him into the wall. His spine cracked, his body jerked with the impact, and Absolon's slavering frothing mouth was close to his. He knew better than to look him in the eyes.

"Sol, please," he said softly. "What happened to you?"

"Liar! Oathbreaker!"

"Yes, Sol, I'm all of it. I'm sorry."

"You did this to me. You cursed me with this."

"I know. I can see it. Let me help you."

Ragnar put a hand on his shoulder, but Absolon snapped his jaws at him and threw Ragnar back against the wall, knocking the air from his lungs. He steadied himself, tried again, shaking, and this time Absolon didn't push him away. A cornered beast, he only wanted to bite, but if he expected to be struck, Ragnar had to make him believe the opposite.

He put his other hand on Absolon's other shoulder, earning a growl from the berserker. Ragnar still didn't look in his eyes, but he felt the hot breath shooting out of Absolon's nose. Slowly, he brought his hands closer together, smoothing along Absolon's shoulders and up to the base of his neck. He stopped, waiting to be thrown off or struck.

Meeting no resistance, his hands slid up Absolon's neck. The berserker bucked. Ragnar held on, shushed him carefully, then hummed *Hitta mig på morgonen*. Absolon bristled but the fit eased. Ragnar's hands grew hot, warmed by the heat of Absolon's blood. Absolon's hands were pressed hard against the wall beside Ragnar's ears, tensing and relaxing and trying to dig their way through the stone. Ragnar continued humming, gliding his hands up to Absolon's burning cheeks. Praying he wouldn't be rejected and punished for his boldness, he looked into Absolon's eyes and sank into the fear and pain filling them.

"Give it to me, Sol. I can take it. All of it." Ragnar carefully touched his lips to Absolon's mouth.

Absolon slammed him against the wall, his mouth mashing painfully against Ragnar's. A wave of sadness washed through him, and Absolon scrambled like he was trying to push through Ragnar. He shuddered, and the berserker fit passed. A heavy, harsh sob erupted from Absolon's throat and lodged in Ragnar's unprotected heart. Absolon cried into his mouth, a bellow followed by tears. Ragnar hugged him close and broke the kiss to whisper close to his ear.

"Give it all to me, Absolon. Give me what I deserve."

Absolon stepped back, wiped his mouth with the back of his forearm, and looked at Ragnar with sorrowful determination. Ragnar didn't change a muscle in his body or face. He barely breathed. The fit had passed, but Absolon was still unstable. One wrong move and any hope he had of turning this to his advantage would shatter. But thoughts of escape drowned as the sweaty mass of Absolon stood before him. Ragnar wanted him more than he'd ever wanted him before.

"Fuck me, Absolon. Fuck me like you hate me."

Absolon charged, grabbed at Ragnar's trousers and ripped them from his body, exposing his already hard cock, and with breathtaking strength, grabbed the chains and ripped them from the wall. How strong was he? But the thought didn't linger as Absolon spun him around, wrestled down his own trousers, and pressed him against the wall. He spat on his cock and pressed it against Ragnar's hole, barely giving him a moment to gather himself before pushing his way inside.

Ragnar cried out silently as Absolon impaled him, a burning that made him hiss and grit his teeth. Absolon was not gentle, but Ragnar took it. He took it all as Absolon drove into him again and again, until pain gave way to his pleasure. He struggled to keep the moans from escaping while Absolon hit the sweet spot deep inside. Absolon was big and riding his cock had always brought him great pleasure, but now, his desperate fucking overrode his silence and he swore aloud as Absolon ploughed him. He begged for more and didn't care that he sounded like a harlot. He pushed back onto Absolon's thick shaft, forgetting this was meant to be for Absolon and Absolon alone. If he were going to die, he wanted his last fuck to be memorable.

Absolon fucked him hard and fast, digging his fingers into Ragnar's hips with such force he'd leave bruises, but for now all pain was good pain. Absolon's breath shortened, hastened, ramming into him for a few good strides, and came with a heart-wrenching guttural cry that left Ragnar's body quivering. Absolon gasped for air and let his head drop onto Ragnar's sweat-soaked back.

They stayed like that, Absolon's cock pulsing inside his ass, making Ragnar's own cock twitch for attention. But he dared not push back and derive more pleasure for himself while Absolon was so still.

Then he heard it. His stillness gave way to trembling, his silence to sobs, and tears soaked into Ragnar's shirt. Absolon wept and the sound and the heaviness of his body weighed on Ragnar's heart, grinding it into pulp. He had done this. He had always thought the worst he could have done was take another's life, yet here was a destroyed man.

A man he had destroyed.

"Sol?"

When there was no change, he repeated himself and Absolon pulled out of him slowly and turned away. Ragnar hated how empty he felt. And though the manacles were no longer attached to the wall, he was in no way free.

"Sol, tell me what happened."

Absolon wiped at his red eyes and sniffed up the snot in his nose. "You don't want to hear it." He tucked himself away.

"I do."

"You'll think I'm a monster."

"I won't, I promise."

Those words: *I promise*. Ragnar had never trusted them himself, and he'd already ruined Absolon's eternal trust in everything; why should he trust him now? But Ragnar gathered the rug around himself to hide his nakedness and sat on the stool, keeping away from the door, away from any potential Absolon might see in him attempting to escape.

"There's nothing you can say that will make this any worse."

Absolon's mouth hitched up in the corner, like it was a joke that Ragnar hadn't been allowed into. "After you tied me up and…and abandoned me, I tried to get free." He put his fingers to his mouth and plucked at his bottom lip. "You…" He blew out a breath. "You broke my heart and…and I thought…" He paused, his gaze flicking to Ragnar then away again. "I thought that once I got free and found you I could…I could make you see your mistake."

He pulled at his lip again like he was trying to drag the words out of his mouth. His eyes looked into the past.

"I still believed that you loved me. I thought it was a test." He bunched his fingers at his mouth, then closed them into a fist. "Or a game, or anything, but the truth was…the truth was you didn't want me anymore."

Ragnar wanted to correct the record but held his tongue.

"When I couldn't get free and when you didn't come back, I went berserk." He closed his eyes and the old shame fell over him. "The fit came and I tried to escape, but it was no use. I collapsed and lost all track of time." He opened his eyes and looked straight at Ragnar. "All I could think of was what had I done to deserve such contempt."

Ragnar shivered and held the blanket tighter. Guilt coated his heart in cold grease; he closed his mouth lest he gag.

"But my yelling brought someone to my side. I became aware of them and thought—hoped—it was you, but it was the Devil. A devil named Lysander."

Absolon leaned against the doorframe and blew out a long breath. "He was refined, like you. Handsome and wicked, like you. He broke my bonds with no more strain than you would have breaking a twig. He held out his hand to me and asked my name and called me beautiful, called me a jewel, and asked me to go with him."

His hands had closed into fists, but noticing this, Absolon opened them and stroked his index finger with his thumb, as if coaxing out the story.

Or poison.

"I said I was grateful for freeing me but there was another I needed to go to. He grew jealous and asked who it was, so I told him. He called me a fool for wanting to go to the one who'd imprisoned me and encouraged me to go with him. At first, I was cautious, but soon his words made more sense and my anger at you grew. Lysander kept me calm, he promised me a way to find revenge, and then he fucked me. He fucked me a lot."

He moved on to stroke the next finger. "He wasn't you, but it was the first time I felt I was the only thing in anyone's world that mattered. I never felt like that with you. I tried to trick myself into believing it, but something else was always more important." He snorted derisively. "And yet I didn't mind. But with Lysander…"

Absolon cracked his neck and continued. "He took me with him. We found a place to stay and I thought I was happy. I tried to put you behind me, but every now and then he would stoke those fires with his jealousy. He thought I deserved revenge, and it didn't take much for me to agree. I wanted to seek you out, but he said there were better paths to revenge, especially ones where I was assured victory."

All movement ceased and Ragnar's heart held.

"He revealed himself. As he truly was. His body glowed beneath the light of the moon like an angel. I couldn't believe my eyes. I thought I'd gone mad, but he told me it was real. That he was special. That he was a thing called a Darisami. It wasn't until later I learned what that meant."

Absolon rubbed at his sternum, kneading into his flesh.

"He took me to a dark part of town, where cutthroats abounded, and told me to watch. Soon enough, we were set upon. The knife flashed and stabbed Lysander. I rushed to avenge him, but he ordered me to stop. He withdrew the blade and the wound closed."

If Absolon spoke true, where was this Lysander now? And how could he find him?

"Lysander said no mortal weapons could hurt him. He said this while he pinned the cutthroat to the wall. He told me he had been alive two hundred years. I said it was impossible, but he pressed his hand against the cutthroat's chest, no easy feat as he writhed for freedom, stilled for a second then the cutthroat stopped moving. Euphoria swept over Lysander's features. I didn't understand what had happened beyond knowing that Lysander had killed the man with his touch."

Anguish plucked at Absolon's face. "The body had barely hit the ground before I ran. Lysander caught me in no time and begged me to listen. He said that the Darisami were soul-eaters, and I could be one too. I'd live forever. I'd have strength beyond mortal comprehension. I'd be immune to sickness and disease. I could have everything I ever wanted." His voice grew agitated and excited as the memories danced across his eyes, lost for a long heartbeat in the moment of his choice.

"I resisted at first, but then I asked why me? He said he was lonely, that he recognized the same wound in me, and he could think of no one better to spend eternity with." Absolon looked at Ragnar. He shrugged his shoulders. "What else was I meant to do?"

A breath exploded out of Ragnar's mouth. "What happened?"

"He turned me." Absolon's words lost their shine; this was now a soldier's report of a battle hard won. "He took my soul into his and gave it back to me. Then I was free from mortal constraints, but it left me with a hunger that has to be sated with one human soul every thirty days. One life per month in order to keep on living."

Surely, it was not possible, and yet Absolon believed it.

"Did he tell you this before he turned you?"

"He did. At least he had the decency to do that. I accepted regardless. I knew what I was getting into even if I didn't understand it. I have killed as a man and it barely affected me, but this… Knowing I must kill someone every month or else I die… It is not easy. It is not easy at all."

"When did this happen?"

"About seven months past."

"Then why did you not come for me sooner?"

"Because Lysander filled everything at that time. My need for revenge had been smothered by his deeds. He no longer angled for me to take your life because he had won me completely. What could you have done to take me from him?"

"So, what happened? Where is he?"

Absolon hung his head. "He grew tired of me. Once the long days of summer passed, his fun was over. With a few harsh words from his scornful tongue, he left, and I have not seen him since."

"Do you miss him?"

Absolon laughed harshly. "I hate him for what he has done to me and for how he has made me different from other men."

"You were always different from other men, Sol. Better too."

"That is no longer true."

"And what about me?"

Absolon shook his head. "Oh, you were the source of all this. Once I had regained myself and banished my self-pity over yet another person abusing me and my trust, I went in search of you, but you were hard to find. It took me a while, but I found you. I didn't attack you at first. I wanted to watch. I wanted to draw it out. Lysander taught me that. He did it to me; he did it to his victims."

He looked ashamed. "I watched you with Åke. I wanted to kill you both in those moments, but I restrained myself. You had replaced me, and it was then that the last buried hope of us ever being together again, of any of your actions being a mistake, shriveled and died. When you returned from that last raid, I struck, and I struck Åke first. You know the rest."

Ragnar slumped, released from Absolon's tale. It could

all be fancy designed to make him doubt his sanity, but the earnestness in Absolon's voice, combined with the few displays of his power that he'd seen, made him believe it was not some fantasy. To think that Absolon possessed so much power... Why, if he had it, there would be no stopping him. But how to get it?

"You're right though."

Ragnar looked up. "I am?"

"What Lysander did to me wasn't your fault, and while I don't think there's a person alive who could say I'm not justified in taking my revenge on you, it won't make things right. In fact, it'll make it worse."

"How so?"

"Because when you take a soul, you have the chance to experience everything in that person's life they've ever felt or done. I don't think I could handle knowing—one way or the other—whether you ever truly loved me, and I wouldn't be able to stop myself from finding out."

"What are you saying?"

Absolon grabbed the keys, took up Ragnar's wrists, and undid the manacles. "I don't want to kill you."

He almost laughed. "Are you sure? This isn't some game?"

"I am not Lysander. And I'm not you."

Ragnar rubbed his wrists.

"I'll get you some new clothes...again...then you can go." Absolon left the cell, leaving the door open, tempting, inviting.

Could he trust it? Could he trust Absolon? Or would he be struck down the second he left the cell? He waited. He couldn't leave anyway, not with his balls flapping in the breeze. And not without knowing more of Absolon's power. He refused to believe in God, but if he did, he'd entertain the notion that divine providence had brought him there and he would have Absolon's gift bestowed upon him. Greatness would be his at last.

Absolon returned empty-handed with a sheepish bent to his body. "I forgot that was the last set."

Ragnar laughed but not too hard in case it offended. "It's fine. The blanket will do for now. Besides, I don't want to leave."

Absolon blinked. "What do you mean? I'm letting you go. You have to leave."

"Is that because you don't want me here?"

Absolon hesitated. "You don't belong here."

He took a few steps closer to Absolon. "What if I want to stay? With you?"

"I'd call you a liar."

"Come on, Sol. Where else am I going to go? I've got no band of brothers left. I haven't even got any clothes. I'm wanted in only God knows how many counties."

"Then why not head for that hoard of plunder you're so proud of?"

"I don't know where I am and with no horse and no provisions and *no clothes*, I can hardly leave right now, can I? Look, you were going to keep me for three weeks more. Why not let me stay while I figure things out?" He let the blanket drop a little. "I'm sure we can make the time pass quickly."

"The whores of Stockholm have nothing on you."

"Is that a yes?"

Absolon's mouth moved like he was sucking on pebbles. "Fine. You can stay, but three days at the most. I'll bring you some straw to make a bed."

Ragnar's eyes bugged. "I'm not staying in this cell, Sol. There must be room in your home for me."

"I might be letting you go, but you still don't deserve

comfort. It's either here, or nowhere. My generosity will extend to keeping this door open."

Every time he thought he could twist Absolon one way, he got twisted around the other. "Very well. Straw it is."

Absolon gave a half-smile, the first sign of merriment in the time he'd been there. He could work with that. A smile from Absolon was as good as any declaration of love, and he'd need as many as he could manufacture if he wanted Absolon to turn him into a Darisami.

ABSOLON FURNISHED HIM WITH AN EXTRA BLANKET AND A
thick mound of straw, but Ragnar had to remain content
with staying naked for the night apart from his boots. Once
the sun started to descend, Absolon refused to go into the
nearest village for fear of exposing himself to moonlight.
Ragnar longed to see that, to have some confirmation of
the supernatural and of Absolon's power beyond what he
had already experienced.

Absolon brought him food but otherwise forbade him
from coming into the farmhouse, small as it was. He said if
Ragnar disagreed, he was welcome to leave, but wolves
had been known in the area and Absolon would not supply
him with weapons.

Ragnar stayed.

Of course he stayed.

He settled into the cell, left the door ajar, and wedged
himself in the corner opposite from where he used to be
bound. The chains stayed where they'd been dropped, a
reminder of his bondage, of his weakness, of Absolon's
power.

Power that would be his.

If it existed.

Absolon had told a good story and there were plenty who would have believed him; most of the dead men in his band for a start. Skogsrå meet Absolon; Absolon meet Skogsrå. A match made in heaven. Or Hell. Or perhaps nowhere. Men had gone mad before and Absolon had ever been treated badly. Perhaps he'd snapped and lost himself in fanciful stories to ease his pain.

Ragnar massaged the center of his chest to smother the dull ache that had appeared during Absolon's tale and not abated. At the least Absolon's strength was something he could turn to his own design. There was no band of bastards left for him to draw upon. Absolon had done him a service in clearing them out. He didn't have to feed them through the winter when the chances of raiding froze. He could stay at the farm through the coldest part of the year, encourage Absolon to join him, and they'd go off again, build up another group of cutthroats. Absolon could be his secret weapon.

And if Absolon were telling the truth—that he was some powerful mystical being who stole men's souls with barely a touch—then Ragnar would take that power for his own.

He chuckled to himself, at Absolon's delusions as well as his own gullibility. A soul-eater? Absolon's mind had shattered along with his heart.

And isn't that my fault too?

He tutted aloud, cursed his conscience back into silence, and sang to ensure it didn't speak again. He still needed Absolon to trust him. He sang Absolon's favorites, starting with the songs of battles won, rousing renditions to stir him from his seat, to inspire him with feelings of camaraderie, of companionship, of joined purpose, and remind him of the good fights when they'd been together.

Next he turned to the bawdy songs, changing them to be not about a fine young lass or a saucy wench, but to a comely lad or a cheeky boy, before dipping into the songs of love and hope.

The glow of Absolon's lantern lightened the doorway.

He would have turned to the slow songs of heartbreak, but he couldn't do it, so eager was he to have Absolon step inside. If he could draw him in with song alone, he could tame the beast and bend him to his will. He leaned against the cell wall, arranged the blankets as seductively as he could, but in the gloom, what did it matter? Absolon's hands would find everything he needed as he always had before.

But Absolon didn't enter. The lantern's glow was sure enough, casting light into the doorway, but he stayed beyond it.

Very well. If Absolon wouldn't come to him, then he would go to Absolon. He could show some deference, some willingness to submit. After all, he enjoyed a good fuck as much as Absolon.

And that last fuck…

Ragnar covered himself and started singing Absolon's new favorite. He stood and draped the blanket over his shoulders, the rest of him as bare as he could endure. He steadied, paused to build up to the chorus, walked out from his corner, around the door and—

Fear gripped his heart and terror congealed in his blood.

"Now you know it's real."

Ragnar blinked. Absolon glowed, not from the light of a lantern, not from the light of a fire, but out of himself as the moon beamed from above. His body radiated light, shining like an angel. But the look on his face reflected only sadness.

He looked so forlorn, so sorrowful, so pathetic, yet all Ragnar could do was freeze and think over and over that this couldn't be real, that Absolon couldn't have told him the truth, because if it were true, then Absolon was as deadly as he said he was.

"I'll bring you some clothes in the morning and you can leave soon after. I understand." Absolon walked away. The light stayed with him because *he was the light.*

Ragnar's mind fought against this impossibility, yet it was exactly as Absolon had described. And if he didn't act fast, he'd lose any chance of having this for himself.

"Absolon, wait." He hurried after him. He hesitated to touch him, wondering if his hand would burn or he'd be turned to a pillar of salt, but he swallowed and pressed on. He held Absolon's arm, grateful that he could stop his hand from shaking and that Absolon could not see all his fear. He held the blanket tighter in case he trembled. "Why are you leaving?"

He scoffed. "I saw the way you looked at me. You're frightened of me, like everyone else."

"I'm not like everyone else, Sol. It's me. Ragnar the Red, remember? You don't scare me."

"Try saying that in a louder voice." He pulled his arm free. "I don't expect you to stay. Good night."

"Stop, will you? Yes, it was a shock, but it doesn't scare me. I am here. I want to stay."

"No, you don't. You have other plans, and if you were as smart as I know you are, you'd be running far from me."

"I'm not going anywhere."

"Not until something better comes along. Stuck here with a monster is not what you want, we both know that. Good night."

Absolon was leaving. Ragnar struggled for the right words to say, searching for an apology or a reason that would hold Absolon to him, but all the talking he'd ever done had never done much. He had to act. He cast off the blanket and ran to Absolon, grabbed his arm hard, and pulled him back. The force was strong enough to turn him, and as Absolon opened his mouth to argue, Ragnar kissed him.

Absolon resisted, his hands coming up to push against his bare chest. His fingers dug into Ragnar's skin, but Ragnar kept kissing, eyes screwed shut, hands going up and into Absolon's hair. He felt so familiar, the same as all those other nights in the dark with nothing else to cling to. Absolon relented, stayed, stunned perhaps, but Ragnar would use whatever he could. His mouth softened, his jaw opened and moved, his tongue searched and stroked, and the kiss expanded, became more than a shield yet not quite a weapon. It was a kiss like the ones of old, the ones of desperate need that had been unlike those he'd ever shared with anyone else.

Absolon's hands relaxed and smoothed around his back, holding him close, but Ragnar was only barely conscious of his touch, lost as he was in the softness of Absolon's lips, and the familiar passion of his mouth. The more he kissed Absolon, the more a gap in his chest opened, releasing a yearning that he had kept locked down for longer than a year. He let it out with a moan into Absolon's hungry mouth.

Coarse hands enlivened his skin like he'd drunk *akvavit*. Absolon led him into the house, laid him on his bed and made love to him with a frenzied but mournful devotion.

RAGNAR WOKE BENEATH THE CRUSH OF HALF OF ABSOLON'S heavy body on him and listened to his gentle snuffling. From the heat in the sparse room, it was going to be a warm day, probably their last until spring came and the flowers woke from their slumber to greet the returned sun. Hopefully Absolon would wake before then.

Ragnar turned his head to get a better look at Absolon's dwellings: a single long room with a hearth at the far wall, two tables and benches, shelves that held dishes and cups, a cupboard mounted on the wall, and a collection of farm tools that gathered dust and cobwebs.

Absolon grew up in something similar though would have shared it with his mother, his two brothers and two sisters. Their father had died of stitch and sting, the ailment in his lungs stealing the man when Absolon was thirteen. What did he think of having all this space to himself?

As for Ragnar, it was barely bigger than the kitchen in his father's castle, though, he had to admit, a damn sight more comfortable than the forest he'd been exiled to. At least this was a home.

He scratched himself, stretched to get some blood flowing into the parts of his body that were going numb beneath Absolon's weight, and stirred him from his rest. Absolon smacked his lips and struggled to open his eyes. Ragnar brushed the white hair out of them and caressed his brow. The lines of worry and age had fallen from his face and he appeared so much like the young man he'd been when they'd first met.

Angelic.

Now more so than ever.

Absolon pried open his bleary eyes. Sleep had fled and been replaced with trepidation and a trace of confusion.

"Good morning," Ragnar said as brightly as he could.

Absolon grunted, threw back the blanket, rolled off the straw-stuffed mattress, and searched for his clothes. He gathered them into one hand.

"What's wrong?" Ragnar asked.

"That wasn't supposed to happen." He hmphed. "Not again."

"I'm glad it did."

"What?" He stopped like he'd been slapped.

"I'm glad it did." He rolled back onto the bed, put his hands behind his head, teasing Absolon with the full display of his body.

"You always were about your own pleasure."

"I wasn't thinking of me."

"That's a first."

"Well, not just me. We were always good at that, and last night was exceptional." *Better than exceptional. Intoxicating and addictive.* "But I thought you needed to relax a little. You're not as much of a monster as you think you are."

"You think because you let me fuck you that means I won't hurt you."

"Do you still intend it?"

Absolon paused then shook his head.

"Then don't worry about it."

"You can't say things are fine and expect them to be so."

"I didn't say *all* things were fine but you, *you* are fine. You don't scare me, Absolon. You are not a monster. And if you want me to leave, then that is your right. This is your place, after all, but…well…if you'll let me, I'd like to stay."

Absolon narrowed his eyes. "Why?"

"Because I want to make amends."

"Since when?"

"Since I saw how broken you were last night." He slid to the end of the bed and placed his feet on the floor. "I know I have no right to expect your forgiveness or for you to give me charity, but I would like to repay you as well as I can for the wrong I've done you."

"You think a few fucks will do it?"

"They can't hurt."

Absolon glowered, but Ragnar laughed. "I'm joking. Though what we did last night would make the nights easier to bear. You can't enjoy so much solitude, and wouldn't I be better than no one?" Ragnar stood and took hold of Absolon's hand. "Let me take care of you for a change."

"I want for nothing."

"Nothing except companionship and care. I can give you that." He silenced the doubt inside himself.

Absolon chewed on his cheek. "I'll think about it. I'm going to wash then I'll get you some clothes from the village."

"Is it far?"

"Not for me and my speed, but for you it would take most of the day."

"I guess I'll stay here then."

Absolon didn't answer, just gave a long, disparaging look at his naked body, and left the room.

Ragnar waited, listening to the splash of water and a few muttered curses before Absolon's feet hit the dirt in a heavy thud. He hurried outside and looked for Absolon but there was no sign of him. He shook his head at Absolon's speed and walked naked to the trough. He scrubbed himself of the dirt and the grime that had clung to him over the past week.

A week...

It had felt like months trapped in that cell wondering what Absolon was capable of. Well, he'd shown him, all right. Shown him intimately. And yet the fear drifted away beneath the full gale force of his ambition. Absolon had power and Ragnar would have it for his own. Then he wouldn't need to rely on cutthroats and bandits to carry him into the hallowed history books. He could perform heroic deeds—truly heroic deeds—by himself alone which would bring him before the King. His father and brother would not be able to dismiss him so easily then. They would cower in fear at his strength and he would be denied nothing.

He rinsed his face and beard, detangled the matted mess of his red hair, and braced against the chill morning air, before returning to the hovel he'd call home for the next few months if all went well. He still had nothing to wear but he put his boots on and wrapped a cloth around his waist. When Absolon returned, he wanted to be ready to fuck him for days if that's what it took. By the time he was through he'd have Absolon panting for him like a dog and willing to perform any trick he commanded.

Thankfully, Absolon had left some food: a few pieces of dried fish and bread that was beginning to turn stale. He grazed on them as he explored Absolon's home, but there was little of interest. Some furniture, a hearth that he tended for his own needs if not for Absolon's, but nothing to make it personal. They'd left the army with nothing and he'd abandoned Absolon with only his clothes; what could he have taken even if he'd had anything?

There was plenty of farm equipment, but it was unused. What did Absolon do there? How did he spend his days? And where were the original occupants? He shuddered to think, but his imagination supplied the horror. One stormy night, the family sitting down to eat... Absolon darkened their door, carried on the back of a nightmare, stole into their home then stole their souls.

One day that would be him.

Ragnar went outside, circled the building, bypassed his former cell, and walked the farmstead, across the uneven ground, refastening the cloth over his hips as needed. The breeze brushed his balls and the wind pinched his nipples, but he gritted his teeth and walked the length and breadth of the field, surrounded on three sides by forest. A stream babbled out of view but to what river it ran, he had no idea. No mountains rose up beyond to indicate where he was or if he were even still in Sweden, though he reasoned that Absolon could not have taken him far from the site of his kidnapping if he remained unconscious throughout the journey. Perhaps they weren't too far at all, and his treasure was within grasp.

He scoffed at himself. What was he worrying about treasure for? He could have the whole of the Empire's treasury if he so wished.

He walked, spotting fresh pawprints in the soil. So, the dog was still lurking nearby. Absolon would be pleased about that, though the fact it hadn't yet returned to the house did not bode well. He dropped a piece of uneaten fish in case the animal was hungry and would return with more when Absolon brought him some. In secret. He didn't want to get Absolon's hopes up.

He kept to the farmed land rather than step into the shade. He preferred being somewhere he could see no confinement, where he was free to roam as far as he liked. He ignored his superstitious fear, infected by all those stories of his dead men. It was better to stay where Absolon could see him when he returned.

Even then, he was unprepared.

"Afraid of the forest, Ragnar?" Absolon said from behind him.

Ragnar cursed and spun, stepping further into the weak midday sun. "Just walking your demesne, Sol."

"It ends somewhere back there, beyond the stream."

"So it is yours then? You bought it?"

"I did." He stepped out of the shadow of oak and spruce carrying a stuffed satchel. "Lysander left behind a lot of possessions. He liked to collect things, jewelry in particular, and when he abandoned me, I sold everything, hoping he'd hear about it and it would bring him pain. I turned away from everything he wanted me to be and became what I'd always said I was—a peasant. I bought this place, hoping it would draw him back. But it didn't. Trogen provided some company, but the silence provided fertile soil for my hate of you to return."

"You have built yourself a fine home."

"Better than the one you and I lived in."

Ragnar shrugged. "That hovel was more of a home than the one I grew up in." And that was the truth. It was where he kept his most prized possessions, along with his most treasured memories. Maybe he'd go back there one day. He pointed at the satchel. "Is that for me?"

Shrugging it off his shoulder, Absolon held it out at arm's length. Ragnar came closer and took hold of the satchel, but when Absolon retreated, Ragnar grabbed for his hand. Absolon froze and looked at Ragnar with the full strength of his sadness. Unwanted, abandoned, cursed. Ragnar told himself he only wanted to twist those feelings to his advantage, but his soul ached to see Absolon so forlorn.

"Come with me." He tugged Absolon towards the line of trees.

Absolon resisted. "You should dress, or you really will die of the cold."

"Later."

He pulled and Absolon followed. The temperature cooled in the shade and Ragnar's skin livened with the brisk wind and anticipation. There was nothing to fear in the trees, not with Absolon there, and soon the magic of the woods opened before him. The smell of damp rich earth, the twitter of birds and the trickle of fresh water… how the place must sparkle in spring!

"Do you remember our first night in the forest after we left the army?"

"Left? You were court-martialed and I deserted, but yes, of course I remember."

"Do you also remember how grateful I was that you were there with me?"

He stopped. "That wasn't gratitude. You were a raging lunatic. Your temper was so bad the animals in that barn thought a storm was coming. I was frightened of you."

Ragnar closed the gap again and steered Absolon until his back was up against a tree. "Is that all you felt? Fear?" Ragnar placed his hand on Absolon's chest and slid it down his muscled abdomen and lower to press against the bulge of his trousers.

Absolon's hand gripped Ragnar's wrist, and Ragnar nearly purred from his might. He bit his bottom lip and held Absolon's gaze with an intense focus that could have burned wood. Despite the hold tightening on his wrist, he was still able to press his palm against the outline of Absolon's thickening cock.

"I would have let you do anything to me then," Absolon whispered.

"And now?" Ragnar sank to his knees, still held, still in Absolon's power. He looked up, determined, strong, in control. "You helped me then. Allow me to help you now. Let me take your pain and swallow it whole."

Absolon's cock twitched, throbbing and primed, having grown beneath Ragnar's attention and the stirring of that remembrance of their first night together in the forest. Both unwanted. Both abandoned. Both cursed.

And both desperate to forget everything that had happened.

Absolon's grip loosened enough to give Ragnar assent, and with his free hand unbuckled Absolon's belt and untied his trousers, letting them drop to the ground to reveal Absolon's erection. Ragnar wet his lips and forgot himself. Forgot that this was all meant to be about tricking Absolon into making him into a soul-eater. Forgot that this was all about power. Forgot all the wrong that Sol had done to him and he had done to Sol.

Instead, it became all about their pleasure.

He took Sol far into his mouth and relaxed his throat to limit his gagging. Even then tears welled in his eyes. He moved his head back and forth, building up a rhythm, with Absolon trying not to thrust but cursing when he did. Ragnar's throat opened wide to take him deep, feeling full, feeling secure and complete with Absolon there. He gripped the shaft with his free hand, using his saliva to make him slick and move in time with his head so Absolon never lost a second of pleasure.

He focused on his other wrist, the one Absolon still held and held so tightly his bones hurt from the squeeze. He could snap his wrist and Ragnar wouldn't care. Absolon's fingers burrowed into Ragnar's hair and gripped him, and no matter how much Ragnar tried to control the motion, Absolon took over, his hips pushing deep into Ragnar's throat. He relaxed and gave himself over completely to Absolon's frenzied thrusting, moaning at the sound of Absolon's groans. His own cock ached to be touched, straining and throbbing in exquisite pain.

And when he thought Absolon was going to punch through the back of his throat, when his scalp sang out in pain, when his wrist creaked close to breaking, Absolon came into his mouth with three hard jolts. Ragnar swallowed his thick offering whole. Absolon spasmed, his breathing labored, then pushed Ragnar away.

Ragnar sat back on his haunches, cock tenting and leaking into the blanket that covered him and licked his lips of anything that had escaped and sucked it into his mouth.

Apart from Absolon's added strength, the experience was exactly the same as that first night in the forest. He'd lost control of so much that he'd needed a way to regain it, and Absolon had been that. He had wanted to give pleasure to know that he could have another man in his power whenever he chose. He needed that confidence, that reassurance, regardless of what he had to do to get it. The fact that he enjoyed sucking Absolon's cock dry was an added benefit.

He didn't stand. He waited until Absolon's breathing had returned almost to normal. He didn't touch himself, no matter how much he ached to. Only when Absolon looked at him, did he speak.

"Will you let me stay? With you?"

Absolon put his cock away and buckled his trousers without taking his eyes off Ragnar. And when he was done, he stalked over, grabbed Ragnar by the throat and hoisted him into the air. Ragnar's eyes bulged in fear. Had he got it wrong? He grabbed Absolon's forearm in some vain attempt to keep himself alive, but then Absolon brought him close and kissed him, long and deep and exploring, his tongue swiping over the thickness of Ragnar's own. Relief swept through him, and he gave himself over.

Absolon broke the kiss abruptly, and Ragnar scrambled to stop his mouth reaching for more. So aroused and yet so helpless, he barely admitted to himself how much he liked it. He opened his eyes to Absolon's smug grin.

"Yes, you can stay."

———

THAT KISS WAS NOT ONE OF CAPITULATION, NOR WAS IT ONE of declared love. Absolon had done it to stamp his control over Ragnar, but if that's what he needed to believe, then Ragnar could go along with it. Absolon needed another's love to survive, and Ragnar could make him believe that's what he was being given. In exchange, he would be made Darisami. All the affection he gave Absolon now could serve as payment, because once he was changed, he'd owe his former lover nothing.

Absolon allowed him to share his bed and in return Ragnar allowed him to use his body, drawing as much pleasure from it as he could without letting Absolon feel anything but in charge. Yet after the second night, he found himself drawing closer to Absolon's body in the cold hours, hugging him from behind and wrapping his arm around as much of Absolon's broad body as possible. He pressed his lips to Absolon's shoulder, and the tension melted away. He didn't shift from it, didn't stop, but he didn't overstep. There was something about those moments that he didn't want to ruin with his plans.

In the dead of night, even his ambition slept.

As for their days, Absolon lacked structure and the farmstead was crumbling into ruin. He existed in a purgatory that befit his existence. Neither alive nor dead, neither human nor angel, neither peasant nor noble yet crossing both. He cared little for work, having no need for food to feed himself, but Ragnar got him into it. He warned that the tax collectors or the priests would come eventually demanding their tithe. Unless he planned on killing every single one in the Empire, he would do well to produce something. He replied sullenly that he would steal what he needed, but there was no denying the glint in his eye that he would have something to fill his time.

At least he had strength to work the farm himself, no matter how others—if they ever came—might grow suspicious. The first day he gently guided Absolon into putting his house in order, while Ragnar cleared out the cell he'd been confined to and repurposed it to what it was originally intended for as a tool shed and store.

He talked to him about what the land could produce. Absolon may have worked his family's farm, but Ragnar had learned from those who swore fealty to his father. Management was what he did best, and Absolon was stronger than any beast of burden. It was too late in the year to plant crops, but the soil could be tilled, and weeds pulled in preparation.

And then there should be stables.

He proposed them on the third day, arguing with Absolon about where they should be and fighting against his flimsy resistance. Absolon loved horses and he could breed fine stallions and mares that the local baron would be proud to sit upon. They would also provide companionship for Absolon once Ragnar had departed. Though he didn't say that.

After his oppositions had been overcome, Absolon dragged him into the forest with an axe and they set to felling trees. Ragnar assisted where he could but Absolon did most of the work, and the air was filled with the sound of trees crashing through the canopy and hitting the ground. Absolon worked like a demon until dusk and the two returned sweaty and grimy and covered in saw dust.

Ragnar felt double his age, but Absolon shone in his vitality. A barbarian like no other, showing no sign of exhaustion, he'd cut all he needed and sawn them into planks and posts. Ragnar asked if he could wash him which quickly led to him getting fucked against the trough. Absolon left him spent and satisfied.

When Ragnar woke the next day Absolon was gone but returned by noon with a bag of nails. He dug the holes for the posts and grew the stables. Ragnar helped; despite Absolon's strength, some things required more than one set of hands.

By the end of the day, the stables had been erected and Ragnar was almost too exhausted to stand. Absolon had no such trouble and helped him to the trough. The strength he displayed on the battlefield was built for short bursts, not for sustained peasant labor. How had Absolon stood it on that family farm? Well, he hadn't, had he? He'd left. In search of better things.

And found Ragnar instead.

Absolon stripped him gently of his clothes and washed him with cold water, running his coarse hands over his skin and proving that not every part of him was exhausted. Absolon smiled and continued washing him, but his strokes slowed and delved to the sensitive parts of him, around his neck, under his arms, his nipples, his obliques and down between his legs. His hand wrapped around Ragnar's cock and he tensed, collapsed his head against Absolon's body as he took the last of his strength, and stroked him into oblivion.

He woke early the next morning with Absolon curled around him. He scooted backwards, deeper into the curves of Absolon's body, slipped Absolon's arm under his, and fell back to sleep.

When he roused again, most of the day had passed and Absolon was gone. He dressed, needing the clothes more than ever now that winter was bearing down on them, and spied Absolon across the field. He waved and Absolon waved back, the light had faded already, the sun nearing its setting. Another day had passed without him noticing.

Another day with Absolon.

And another day when he hadn't achieved his goal. He looked at the stable and saw what they had built together. He imagined it filled with horses, imagined the fields filled with barley, and the days passing in toil and his life slipping away in this strange domesticity. It seized him by the throat and warned him not to get complacent.

The Darisami wandered over and when he reached him, he was smiling. He bowled him up into his arms and kissed him. The grip on Ragnar's throat tightened even as he lost himself in that kiss, in the freedom of it, in the love of it.

Absolon broke the kiss but for how long it had ensorcelled him, he didn't know. "I thought you could do with some rest." He didn't unwrap his arms from around Ragnar's waist.

"I didn't realize I was so tired."

He chuckled. "You nobles aren't used to hard work."

And despite the word hitting Ragnar's back teeth, he laughed too. Genuinely.

It could be so easy to stay and give himself to Absolon totally. But there would always be this difference between them: Absolon's strength and immortality versus Ragnar's weakness and ageing. And as wonderful as it was to be in Absolon's arms, it couldn't last. He wouldn't be satisfied with this for the rest of his days, no matter how easy. Absolon would know it too. And perhaps that's where the bargain could be struck.

"I've been thinking." He untangled himself from Absolon's arms and instantly regretted the loss of his body's warmth. "What happens as I grow old and you stay young? Won't that be—"

"No!" The word fired from Absolon as if it had been shot from a musket.

"What? What's wrong?"

"I know what you're asking, and I will not curse anyone else with this." He stormed into the house.

He was smarter than he gave him credit for. "Hear me out, Sol." Ragnar chased after him. "It wouldn't be a curse. It would be a kindness, for you and for me."

He scoffed. "You think I'd enjoy it? That I'd like to make another such as I, another such as Lysander? We're monsters and there should be none of us, not more."

"Then why are you still here? If you think yourself so wicked, why not end it when your thirty days are up?"

Absolon turned away to tend the hearth fire.

Ragnar approached and smoothed his arms over Absolon's thick shoulders. "It's fine, Sol. No man wants to die, least of all me, so I understand why you haven't let death come for you, but why not give yourself some plea-sure? Why not make the years ahead easier?"

"My guilt is forever."

"Then share it with me."

"You don't understand what it's like."

"I've taken men's lives before. I know the horror that can come with it, but it can be soothed. The nights can be filled with love and laughter, not horror and screams. I would stay with you as long as I could, but old age will eventually take me from you, and then who will be there to remember you as you were?"

"You are silver-tongued, that is certain, but you would hate me for what I would do to you."

"I think not. You are not Lysander. You will not do what you think is wrong. You will not abandon me. Think of it, the two of us together, untouchable, unconquerable, living the life we want with no one to ever tell us what to do." Though Absolon always liked to follow orders. "Please, Sol. I do this willingly, knowingly. I want this so I can be with you always."

The words flowed out of his mouth and they came so easily he could have mistaken them for truth. He ignored the desperation in his heart.

Absolon sighed and stared into the fire. He stayed like that for a long time. Ragnar's tongue yearned to speak and press his case further, but the quiet intensity of Absolon's pose told him that speaking was not needed. He waited.

"I'll think about it."

Ragnar smiled and kissed the top of Absolon's head. Absolon's hand found his and they stayed together, warming by the fire while outside a harsh wind whistled and whipped the land.

❧   6   ❧

THE MORNING HAD STOLEN ABSOLON FROM THEIR BED, AND the afternoon did not return him. At first Ragnar thought it possible Absolon had merely gone for a walk in the forest but, as the hours stretched with no sign of him, that idea lost all credence. Perhaps Absolon had gone to the village again for supplies.

He had been left alone before and Absolon had returned, but as the sun passed its zenith and continued to its rest, he was forced to hunt out his own food, catching a hare and cooking it over the hearth. He left a leg out for the dog and stood inside the doorway while he ate, watching across a moonlit fallow field for sign of Absolon's returning glow. He stayed until even the moon had gone to bed.

He slept badly, listening for any sound of Absolon, but he was rewarded with nothing but the wind and an owl's mournful warning. Had Absolon abandoned him? Had his request proved too much and now the soul-eater had gone in search of another home, one far from Ragnar and his petition? Had Absolon seen through his self-serving demand? Then why not stay and tell him no? Why not banish him, or take him to someplace far from here from which he could not return? Absolon had that power.

The next day was no different except for the tension thickening in Ragnar's neck and shoulders. He was a fool. He'd pushed Absolon too far too fast. He should have waited until midwinter. That would have given him more time to ply his honeyed words to make it appear like Absolon's idea all along. He had been too eager for it. Nothing to do with wanting to hide from that look in Absolon's eyes, the one that wanted and believed Ragnar could give him so much more.

Heroes always had to make the hard choice, and this was his. A thousand years could pass in this enchantment, and the world would move on and forget about Ragnar the Red. Time would take his enemies and rob him of his triumph. Then there'd be no place for him in hallowed halls. What kind of life would that be?

He would stay a while longer. He couldn't disprove that Absolon was not nearby, watching him, seeing what he would do when he was on his own. He'd show that he would stay, that he was genuine, that he waited for Absolon and not for Absolon's power.

So he chopped firewood for the stockpile. He oiled the tools. He went far enough into the forest to reach the stream and caught fish for his dinner.

And he waited at the door for Absolon to return.

What would it be like to stay forever?

A bitter wind answered and cut him to the marrow.

The slamming of the storeroom door brought him out of his somber musings. He stalked off to investigate and met Absolon coming around the corner. The moon blessed him, and he shone with the light of a hundred souls. The magnificence of the sight stole Ragnar's breath. If he were a religious man, he would have fallen to his knees and praised the heavens.

But he was not a religious man and he had no use for God.

Still, he would fall to his knees before Absolon.

Absolon almost walked into him, lost in his own thoughts.

"Where were you?" Ragnar asked.

"I had to…do something." He pushed past him and washed his hands and face in the trough.

"I thought you might have left me for good."

"Only you would do that, Ragnar." He went into the farmhouse and dried his face on a cloth, while his accusation dripped into the cold pit of Ragnar's stomach. "I thought about what you asked."

"And?"

Absolon threw the cloth on the table and stood with a hand on his hip. "You need to understand that this is not something to be done lightly, that it turns you into something that even I don't fully understand. The hunger to feed on souls can be…"

"I understand. It can be difficult."

"No, that's not it." He sank onto the edge of the table and expelled a heavy breath. "It's easy. It is so easy." He shook his head at the marvel of it. "At first you think you can't do it and that it will disgust you, that you'll never do it again, but it's almost impossible to stop. There's a hunger in you that's never quite sated, and it tells you that you want to do it, that you want to take that soul and feel it inside you." He licked his lips. "And when you do, there's sadness, but there's also joy, and there's anger, and hate, and fear, and love, and every single thing that person has ever felt passes through you. And once it's in there, you are filled with a divine ecstasy." He paused. His eyes shimmered. He tilted his face to the heavens. "And once it's done, you regret it, but you want it again and you know you'll have it."

"That sounds familiar," Ragnar chuckled.

"This is not funny, Ragnar." He bared his teeth. "This is life and death and it is inescapable."

"It always has been."

"But for you, now, you can choose *not* to kill, *not* to take a life. You can live a life where you do not harm another. Do this, and you have no choice but to kill or die."

His heart stilled, frightened of beating lest it scare Absolon away. What would it be like to feel that power?

"It is no different for me. I would have it. I would be what you are so I may ease your burdens as well as my own. I would share the winters and the summers with you. It would be like it was before, the two of us against the world."

Absolon stood, his hand opening and reaching for him but closing in a fist, too scared to touch. "But it could be that way now, without me doing this, without me cursing you." He slumped back onto the edge of the table.

"It would not last. I would age and weaken, and you would grow tired of my humanity." Ragnar took up his hands. "You would resent my need to eat ordinary food. You would be shamed by my growing infirmity, and I would be jealous of your youth and strength. We would become enemies and you would take my life and damn yourself for eternity."

Absolon sighed and let Ragnar hold him. He rested his forehead against Ragnar's shoulder and enfolded him in a tight, strong embrace. He hugged him with his sorrow and his love. At first it warmed Ragnar's heart, but then it grew too hot and scorched him.

He will never forgive me for what I do to him.

But it was unavoidable.

"I want this, Absolon. I want it so we can be together forever."

Absolon looked up. "I hate how much I want this too, how selfish that makes me, because you hear my words, but you do not know what it means to be what I am."

"Then allow me to make that choice. Your soul will be clean, the damnation is mine, but you will be here to make it all the sweeter."

Absolon shook his head, a small sad smile on his lips. Ragnar leaned down, lifted Absolon's chin and with a gentle kiss sealed his fate. He rubbed his thumb across Absolon's cheek and smiled brighter than Absolon in the moonlight.

"Please, Sol. I want this."

Absolon nodded. "Just remember I warned you, please, and don't hate me for it."

"Never." He kissed him again, his lips buzzing with the anticipation flooding his blood. "How do we begin?"

He took a deep breath. "I will take your soul, pass it through mine, and return it to you different from before. I don't know how the magic works, but that's the process as near enough as I remember."

"Near enough?"

He shrugged. "Lysander told me how, but the steps were vague."

Ragnar felt fear for the first time. "You're not inspiring confidence here, Sol."

"Don't worry. You'll understand once it's over how it's hard to go wrong with this, or anything we do. There are certain symbols and they feel *right*. They're just *there*." He sighed again. "You'll understand when it happens to you."

"And what about after that?"

"There'll be pain. Lots of it—for you, not me—and

then you'll need to feed. I don't know how long after but it's best to do it soon."

The storeroom…

He turned towards it.

"Yes. I found someone already. You will have to take their life in cold blood or lose your own. Can you do that?"

He paused. Of course he could. Couldn't he? But if he couldn't, then that would be his escape. If it proved as horrific as Absolon tried to make it sound, and he could not accept his new nature, he would refuse to feed and go willingly to his death. Wouldn't he?

He nodded, rather than risk uttering those thoughts. Energy thrummed through his body. All that strength. All that light. All that power. A great and glorious future unfurled before him. Nations would tremble. The world would be his.

"Now or never, I suppose," Absolon said. "It's better if you lie down." He led Ragnar to the bed, took off his boots and his coat, and tended to him like he was preparing a corpse. He undid the cords at his shirt and settled his hand onto Ragnar's chest. Heat pressed onto his skin and Absolon's hand weighed heavy on his heart.

"I hope you'll forgive me for what I'm about to do." Absolon's sadness poured off him in waves. This was meant to be a happy occasion but…

What if Absolon had no intention of making him into a Darisami? What if he was going to kill him instead?

Absolon's hand burned his flesh. It had begun. Fast. Like an arrow shooting through him that hooked onto his soul.

My soul.

He had never contemplated it fully before, never ruminated that there was even such a thing as a soul, a part of him inside the rest of the meat and blood and bone that kept him alive. If someone had asked him to describe it, he would have been unable to find the words and struggle to say with any certainty it existed.

But whatever Absolon had done, it defined the length, breadth, and width of Ragnar the Red's soul. The magic caught it, and it flailed. Doomed. He panicked. He knew, instinctively, primally, that if Absolon took his soul, he would die.

Absolon dragged it from Ragnar's body, and the pain arched his back. Iron nails pushed through his veins and he strained against the agony. He raised up off the bed, his neck bulged, his teeth clenched, and toes curled. He grabbed Absolon's hand. He had to stop it, but he could do nothing more than hold on to Absolon's stillness. He was irrevocably within Absolon's power.

White obliterated his mind and he lost all consciousness of what happened next. His soul was torn out and threshed. But then his soul was back as if it had never been taken and he was alive. But something was different.

Very different.

Something had been added. His soul was now something greater than it had been. And when he opened his eyes, Absolon's hand was no longer pressing down on him, but the burn remained like a bright day's afterglow.

He opened his mouth to ask what had happened, but as he met Absolon's sad eyes he stopped.

"It's not over yet."

A great chasm opened in the bottom of Ragnar's stomach, creating a vortex that dragged into it everything that he was. Down and down and on and on until he had been turned inside out. He may have screamed. He may have howled. He could have died and not known. He curled in on himself, pulled his knees up to his chest and waited for birth and death to end.

Then, without him doing anything, because there was nothing he could do, it passed, and he could think again. He could open his eyes again.

He was alive.

"How do you feel?"

His mouth was dry and his throat raspy. He struggled to speak. "Like I've been hanged, drawn, and quartered. Is there more?"

Please, let there be no more.

"That's the ritual over. You'll hurt for a while, but..." Absolon sighed. "But the next part will make that easier." He stood and made a torch from the hearth. "We should get this over with. I don't know how long you'll have otherwise."

He felt fine. He felt powerful, vital, like he'd plunged through an ice hole and come out refreshed. His hands tingled, jostling the growing hunger in his belly. He'd eaten only a few hours earlier and should have been sated, but that chasm within him had not fully closed and demanded to be filled.

Something flickered at the edge of his attention and it made him stumble. Ragnar tried to focus on it, but Absolon clicked his fingers.

"Come."

He followed Absolon outside. He wanted to walk into the middle of the field and dance with the light of the moon pouring out of him, but heavy clouds had rolled in covering the sky.

Later.

Absolon led him around the side of the house. The nearer they got to the storeroom, the more he heard the sound of muffled shouting. Absolon stopped at the door. The key was already in the lock. Waiting. He put his hand on the wood and turned to Ragnar.

"This is it. Take his soul and the ritual is complete. You'll be as I am. If you don't, you will die, but that may be preferable."

"How do I do it?"

"Trust the symbol that is even now coming to life inside your mind. Think it, draw it, sing it if you want, but it must be complete. Touch his bare skin and his soul will be yours. Draw it in as slow or as fast as you wish, like taking a breath."

The hunger had grown. And when he turned his attention inward, a jumble of lines and shapes flickered in the gloom. His breath shortened in expectation; his heart throbbed with need. All he had to do now was take one soul and the rest would fall before him.

"I'm ready."

His face grim, Absolon hesitated before unlocking the door and opening it inwards. The light landed on—

"Åke?"

Ragnar stared at bruised and bloodied Åke lying bound and gagged on the ground. He bellowed through the rag stoppering his mouth and writhed trying to break his bonds.

Ragnar turned to Absolon, his breathing short and fast.

Absolon could not look at him and instead stared into the distance like a statue. "You're not the only one who can be cruel, Ragnar. Now take his soul or die."

Åke's screams increased and pierced Ragnar's chest like poisoned darts. Even though the sound was muffled, he could clearly hear his name pleading in Åke's mouth. He could blame Lysander for birthing such heartlessness in Absolon, but he knew where true responsibility lay.

As you sow, so shall you reap.

He staggered towards Åke and the symbol formed.

Swirling and coalescing like a skittish sprite, he traced its lines, knowing which one to do first, which curve to follow next, until it formed a complete whole of unimaginable power.

The key to unlocking the soul of his enemies.

And of those he could have loved.

But love was a weakness that couldn't be allowed to survive.

He knelt beside Åke and stared into his beseeching eyes. Why couldn't he be some villain? Why couldn't he be someone unknown? He looked back at Absolon and understood, as much as he didn't want to. This was Absolon's revenge, and he would take his punishment.

He stroked Åke's cheek and stared into those confused eyes. The hunger sharpened, slicing him open, demanding something to stop the pain. He would die of that hunger if it weren't sated.

"I'm sorry," he whispered. His hand splayed across the naked flesh of Åke's throat. The symbol flashed in his mind, formed, and catapulted down his arm into Åke's body. He had no control over it, so fervent was it to be free and at its dreadful purpose.

The boy jerked, froze, and Ragnar breathed in his soul as it travelled up his arm. Tears clogged his throat but that didn't stop the soul tickling and tingling along its final journey. He startled and let go, ashamed of what he'd done, but still the soul continued over the distance and along the same path. Ragnar scooted away from the dying body as more of the soul entered him. He backed into Absolon's legs and could go no further.

"Take it in, Ragnar. Take it in quickly so you don't have to see what he was."

Ragnar relaxed and drew on it faster. It filtered through his mind and into his soul, bringing with it awful knowledge. Åke Klimson who had loved Ragnar the Red—

Ragnar jerked, and the soul jumped into him, and Åke's life passed in a blur. He shielded his mind until the soul was in him and the energy exploded into stars. He collapsed against Absolon's legs. His whole body tingled and, through him, rolled a divine ecstasy that obliterated sorrow.

"It is done."

He looked up with drunken eyes at solemn Absolon, but even Åke's sense of betrayal could not keep the grin from Ragnar's face.

Oh, it was glorious, this magic, this feeling, all from taking one soul. He was invincible. His strength restored, his mind cleared, he was stronger and more alive than in any other moment in his life. He bounded to his feet, bursting with the pleasure of it all, with the power of it all, grabbed Absolon's hand and pulled him along—he could now, he was that strong—out into the field where the clouds had parted and the moon shone down. As it lay down its benediction, they glowed.

He held up his hands to the light and laughed at how it streamed out of him, how it made him and Absolon glimmer. He spun with the glory of God. He leapt into Absolon's arms and thanked him with a gratitude that was not faked. And he kissed Absolon, deep and long and hungry, stoking the fires of their passion.

When his kisses became more insistent, when the need for more grew sharper, he drove Absolon into the house and rode him with the ferocity and vigor of a hundred rutting stallions and christened his rebirth with an exultation that Heaven envied.

❧ 7 ❧

THE SUN HAD RISEN MANY HOURS EARLIER WHILE RAGNAR and Absolon stayed abed, fucking languorously through the morning. Ragnar reveled in their stamina and yielded to the sensual pleasure of body on body, of Absolon's rigid yet pliable form beneath him, and brought him to climax again and again.

The morning passed.

Absolon nestled against Ragnar's side, brushing his fingertips through the hair on Ragnar's chest. But the circling of his finger, the drawl of his hand across his skin, was like a spoon stirring a pot of bubbling agitation. Absolon weighed on him. One of Ragnar's arms draped over Absolon's shoulder; the other he kept by his side, locked in a fist.

"When can we go to the village?"

Absolon tilted his face up to him. "Why do you want to go to the village?"

"To look around, to see where I am, to try out my power."

Absolon raised himself, the look on his face uncertain, wary. "You…you want to kill someone?"

"No, not especially, I want to see how much strength I have."

He frowned. "You know you don't have to harvest again for another thirty days."

"What about you? Won't you have to feed sooner?"

He hung his head. "Yes."

"Then we'll go together. We'll put ourselves in harmony."

"Perhaps not today."

Ragnar held back a growl. "How about we stretch our legs and run? I'd like to see how much strength is in me. I saw you moving those tree trunks around; I want to try something similar."

"I guess we can do that." He leaned down and kissed Ragnar's lips, but the action angered Ragnar, provoking a belligerent streak that could not be so easily calmed.

If he wanted to go to the village, who was Absolon to tell him otherwise? Who was anyone to say what he could not do? He was meant to lead, to dominate, to control. He released that fire into the kiss he returned to Absolon and pushed him onto his back, his cock raging to life and rubbing against Absolon's stomach. He broke the kiss to see that smile back on Absolon's face, a corresponding passion in his eye, and an erotic tilt to his off-kilter grin. Ragnar flipped him so he wouldn't have to see that look of love and fucked him until the sun past its peak.

When they finally separated, Ragnar got out of bed and washed himself of Absolon's smell and seed and dressed ready to explore. But Absolon stayed abed, hugging his bent knees, and studied him.

The attention prickled the skin on his neck. "Why are you looking at me like that?"

"What was it like to take Åke's soul?"

His gut twisted on itself, but he forced it to untangle. He would not feel guilt and he would not allow Absolon's act to weaken him. "Bearable."

Absolon shook his head. "You are cruel, Ragnar." He threw back the blanket and marched out of the house to wash.

Ragnar pursued him. "It wasn't I who brought him here. You're the one who made the devil's choice."

"And one fitting for a devil." He scrubbed himself, hurried and rough. "Do you have no remorse for taking his life?"

"Why should I? I gave him peace. What future did he have?"

He stopped and put his hands on the edge of the trough. The muscles in his forearms tensed. "But he loved you and would have done anything for you."

"And he gave the greatest sacrifice so that I may live. I would expect it of any who followed me."

Absolon straightened. "You didn't even try to save him."

"Why would I? He served a much better purpose in giving up his life."

"You honestly believe that people should be grateful they can help you in your aims."

"It is my due. My glory is their glory."

Absolon laughed. "Is that how you see it? As service to the legend of Ragnar the Red?"

"They should be grateful for it. What other meaning would their lives hold? None of them ever actually love me, anyway. Åke never loved *me*, just the idea of me."

And my family didn't even love that.

"And what about me?"

"What about you?"

Absolon stared at him. Waiting.

"What?"

Absolon sighed. "Nothing." He walked away.

"Sol, what is it? If you want my thanks, you have it, but I won't feel guilty about Åke's death."

"Of course not. Ragnar the Heartless never feels guilty about anything." He entered the house, leaving Ragnar with a sick feeling bubbling inside his stomach. Could Absolon really be upset that he'd killed Åke?

Absolon reappeared.

"Why didn't you kill Åke in the forest when you first took him?"

Absolon blinked. "I had an idea that I could use him to wring some remorse from you."

"And are you satisfied?"

He grimaced and bade him lead on. He kept that disgruntled look, like Ragnar had missed something important. It riled him. He should be pleased there were now no rivals for his affection. Ragnar forged ahead.

They sprinted into the forest, and he forgot about the chains fastening around his chest that wanted to bind him to this shitty farm. He instead celebrated the speed bestowed upon him. He'd already had a taste of it in the speed and force with which he fucked Absolon, but this was something else.

The ground and the wind did not hamper him, and they were deep inside the forest before he realized. He hollered with joy and ran farther and faster. He used his speed and strength to jump high into the oak trees like a squirrel bounding through the canopy, and when he landed on the ground, it trembled with the force of his impact but left him untouched. He grinned.

He dug up large boulders like they were pebbles and hurled them into trees that then crashed to the ground. He lifted their trunks above his head. He had to apply his strength, but he was infinitely stronger than he had once been. There would be limits, he could feel that in the strain of his muscles, but they were beyond anything in creation would require.

Such power!

Absolon let him run, let him break things, watched and eventually laughed while he played. By the time he'd grown weary of it, the forest looked like a giant had stormed through and laid waste to the land in search of children to eat. He laughed, a harsh sound that cut out of his chest and throat and cackled into the destroyed grove. There was nothing he could not do.

"What's so funny?" Absolon appeared at his side.

"Just how easy this all is." He cupped Absolon's head in his hands. "To think what we can do. Is there more? What else did Lysander tell you? What else have you learned?"

Absolon took hold of Ragnar's wrists and pulled himself free. "I've learned that it gets lonely." He kissed the palms of Ragnar's hands. "But you're here now."

Absolon looked at him expectantly, but Ragnar could not utter the words he knew Absolon wanted to hear. He didn't know why.

"Come. Tell me what else you know of our kind." He took Absolon by the hand and led him slowly back through the forest so they could talk, and so Ragnar could learn all he had to before he left for good.

Absolon slept soundly, cuddled against Ragnar, a great lump of man that had grown too heavy for him to handle. The afternoon and evening had passed with their discussions, of the limits that Absolon had found to their power, the pain that touching gold brought, the ability to alter the age of one's appearance, and of testing the symbols that flashed for attention inside their minds. They were instinctive yet they still needed coaxing and studying for him to feel confident in them.

There was the one he already knew well—the harvest symbol—and there was the one for making another Darisami, as well as one for the splitting of a soul to allow communication between two Darisami. Beyond those three he couldn't be certain.

Still, those three were enough to define the rest of eternity. He drew them over and over in his mind like a litany, a silent act of devotion to whatever had molded him into this wondrous form. He wondered if there were more symbols and why they had not revealed themselves fully formed in his mind. But this curiosity was not enough to overwhelm the feeling that he had to leave.

He could not have slept even if he'd wanted to. Absolon's face and body had lost the tension they'd held throughout his captivity and freedom. He was again the eager, doe-eyed boy who had first caught Ragnar's eye and the attention of his cock and heart. Absolon touched him more often, freed from any fear of reprisal from the outside world or from Ragnar. There were no proprieties to observe, no shame to keep them hidden, except from the moon, but so far from civilization were they that even that was not a real concern.

Ragnar's skin burned wherever Absolon touched him, a fire fed with unlimited fuel, and he touched the berserker more as well, a stroke to his inner thigh, a hand on the back of his neck, absent-mindedly caressing and laughing and talking and loving—

He swung out of bed and put his feet on the floor. Absolon stirred but rolled over and went back to sleep. Ragnar couldn't stay one day more because one day Absolon would see that he was not worthy of all that his heart had to give. Absolon would know, if he didn't already, what Ragnar had always wanted to deny: that he was useless. He had to prove that it was not so, and he couldn't do that by staying here.

An owl hooted in the still night, catching Ragnar's attention. A call of the wise. He knew the choice he had to take, and once taken it drove him from the hovel with its small room and shrinking walls and as far as he could get before Absolon woke and his resolve broke.

He kept to the shade of the forests in case the moon revealed his presence and gave rise to rumors of an angel in their midst. He pushed his legs to run faster, wondering if Absolon was looking for him and pleading for him to come back.

A village appeared before him, one of reasonable size, but one he didn't know from his limited experience. Was this the village Absolon had come to for his food and clothes? Did they know him there? Was he that isolated, elusive man living alone on that farm? Was he a source of gossip among the women? An object of praise or ridicule among the men? He couldn't think of that or else he'd want to kill everyone in the village.

The need to feed—a beast to rival the dragon Níðhöggr—knew there were souls within reach and wanted to hunt. Is that why Absolon kept himself distant? Because it was so hard to abstain? Well, he would learn to master his hunger and rule over thousands. Millions! But he would not destroy this village in case it was Absolon's field to reap.

Besides, what were these people to Ragnar? They were as nothing. No, his quarry lay much farther afield. Careful to avoid the light of the moon, he stepped out enough from the line of trees to scan the sky and find Polstjärnan. His old garrison and the generals that oversaw them were stationed north; he would head there. He set his course and ran through the night, but the further he got from Absolon, the more his mind stayed back in that farmstead.

When dawn broke, Absolon would know he had gone. Ragnar slapped his thoughts away from dwelling on Absolon's misery. It was necessary. What he was doing had to be done or else there'd be no hope for his future. He could not have stayed with Absolon while this ate away at him.

He ran.

When the night passed, he checked his course at the first village he encountered. The bakers were already at their work and the smell of rye rumbled in his stomach, but he desired only the men's souls, not their wares.

He kept his distance, the symbol flaring in front of his mind when he got too close. He must have looked a bedraggled and ravenous wolf at that moment. The bakers stepped back. One offered him a loaf fresh from the oven, mistaking him for some beggar desperate for food. Ragnar thanked him for his kindness but refused and kept back. He asked for directions and, as soon as he had confirmation he was on the right track, he left.

He hadn't killed anyone, but he wanted to. He could have. Could have done it easily and no one would have stopped him, but he wanted his hunger sharp when he met those who had done him wrong and made him feel lesser. He wanted their souls to be the first to mark his new ascendance.

He forced himself to forget Åke's soul.

He reached the city by the next day's end and when the garrison rose before him, he salivated. He skirted around its high walls to the rear and, when no one was watching, scaled it like a lizard. He traversed the parapet and dropped onto the ground on the other side without detection.

The smell of gunpowder and male sweat wafted into his nose and stirred his longing for that life of war. He had found his place in the military. He walked through the barracks as he had then, confident and assured, despite his shabby dress and lack of uniform. He had risen through the ranks with speed and surety. They had hailed him a hero after one successful battle after another, and his strategies and tactics had been inspired. Even if his father could not fail to give him grudging respect, even if he never said it aloud. They had to take notice of him then, when he brought such glory for Sweden.

All until the battle when he'd lost five hundred men. It had been a gamble, a bold move to rout the enemy, but the men had lacked discipline, and the generals and other officers had quailed and cost them the element of surprise. And he had paid the price for their foolishness.

Ordinarily officers would not suffer such shame—lives were expendable. But it was a step too far for the generals who had been afraid of Ragnar's popularity. They had seen an opportunity and acted, and they had got his father to go along with them. Not that the old miser would have needed much coaxing. His indifference had been locked in decades ago.

General Lundgren had been the one to instigate it, and it was outside his office that Ragnar found himself. His secretary was out, and he marched up to the door bearing the general's name. It was the same as when he'd left but the feeling of looking at it was different. Then he'd been ordered to appear, flanked by guards, but his confidence had been such that he believed he would have nothing to answer for. But now, he knew there was nothing the general could do to stop him.

He knocked and a gruff voice commanded him to enter.

The white-haired general with his thick moustache sat hunched over his desk, quill scrawling rapidly across parchment. Orders for the field, or merely missives to the King, that desk had been where he'd written to his father to ask approval to dismiss. The two old men knew each other, had been friends once, and shared a mutual distaste for Ragnar over what he would have liked to believe was their fear of him but was more likely their ridicule.

Ragnar shut the door and approached the desk. The light in the room was starting to fade despite the candles.

The general took in the shabby clothes covering his

body, curled his lip and smiled when he recognized Ragnar. He put down his quill and leaned back, folding his hands over his stomach.

"I thought you were dead. You certainly look as such. How did you get in here?"

"No defenses can keep me out."

"Well, I suppose whores manage to find their way in here all the time. You'd be no different." The general smirked, superiority oozed out of him. "What do you want?"

"I've come to take my revenge."

Lundgren snorted, leaned over his desk, and waved him away with his hand. "You're lucky we let you out of here alive after your ineptitude, and you dare show your face here? The shame should have kept you away longer than a year. Better men would have drunk themselves to death. Get out." The general picked up his quill.

Dismissed and disregarded, Ragnar's blood boiled and incinerated the calm demeanor he had wanted to project. He reached across the table, grabbed Lundgren by his shirt front, and hurled him across the room. The general's shout of alarm broke short as he slammed into the wall and crumpled to the floor.

Ragnar stalked over to the wincing, grunting figure. Lundgren tried to right himself and regain his composure, but he was flustered. The general raised his arm to protect himself, but Ragnar snared it in his grip and twisted sharply until the bone snapped. The general cried out and fear widened his eyes and mouth.

"What is this?" he stammered.

Ragnar crouched, pressed his hand against the general's chest like an immovable weight crushing him against the wall. He kept up a slow, growing pressure, feeling his sternum and ribs creak as agony twisted his face. "I had to live in the forest for a year. I had to become a bandit, an outlaw, because of what you did, because you thought I was useless."

"You were responsible for the death of five hundred men and your recklessness would have killed a thousand more."

"That number pales compared to the number you have sent to their slaughter. You destroyed my life, and I will repay you in kind."

"I only did what was right. If you want someone to blame, blame your father."

"I will."

Ragnar's eyes flared, he grabbed Lundgren by the throat. The symbol flashed in Ragnar's mind and shot out to do its awful work. The general's soul detached—he could feel the separation, like a click, like a lock unlocking —then it was his. He drew it in, drew it in slow, as slow as he could, to keep Lundgren alive as long as possible.

All the while the general kept his gaze fixed on Ragnar's. He would know to his last breath Ragnar's might. He relished the dread that knowledge invoked and let the general's life wash through him. He caught glimpses of himself, but he was too much in haste and once sighted they were already gone. He searched for more but there were none until his final moments, tarred with terror at what this *thing* had done.

Life left the general's eyes and he slumped like a sack of barley. The energy from the soul barreled through him, rolling and tumbling, and Ragnar stood, breathed deep of his vanquished foe's essence. He flexed his hands and fingers and stretched. Lightning struck his heart, a feeling of being alive, of being vital and connected.

He had been right to choose the general for his first kill. He had got the vengeance he had wanted and ignored

Lundgren's lies. He had not been responsible for those deaths. He had done the right thing and would have brought greater glory for Sweden and the King. But the small-minded fool hadn't seen that, and he'd paid for his mistakes with his life. He cracked his knuckles and went in search of the other men who'd been party to his betrayal.

By the time he was finished, six souls swam through his blood and he swayed like a drunkard. An alarm was raised as he left the barracks dressed in new civilian clothes and a heft of *riksdaler* in his pocket. He longed to take a regimental sword with him, strip the badges from the dead's jackets and take them as trophies, but what did he need with their mortal decorations? He would be praised with sagas. Once he was done with his revenge. Then it could all start afresh.

He turned for the road to Jönköping and his ancestral home. It took him the greater part of the night to reach the outskirts of the city, and he waited for it to stir. He sauntered in, found a room where he could wash and a tailor that could deck him in fine clothes for when he presented himself to his father. He pressed the tailor to have it finished for the next morning, paid him handsomely for it with stolen coin, and spent the hours circling the castle where his father and brother lived. He poured his ire into it, hoping it would catch fire with the strength of his hate alone.

Blame your father, the general had said.

Everything that had gone wrong could be traced back to that odious serpent. His elder brother had benefited from his accident of birth, but there had been more than enough wealth to go around. Everything he had got he had earned for himself, a noble name not counting for as much as it should, and still he was not worthy enough to be treated as an equal son. And after the failed battle he'd been left homeless, without title and without income.

Not that it mattered now.

He forced himself to believe that it didn't matter now.

He could have anything and everything he wanted. But first, he'd kill his father then his brother, and he'd take their place as lord and master. It felt right. It felt divine.

Then maybe there'd be a place for Absolon.

He hissed at the unwelcome thought. Absolon didn't belong in a castle. He would not like it.

Neither did Ragnar, but he would endure it for as long as he needed. He would use it as a base from which to conquer lands and kingdoms. Absolon didn't belong in all that.

It was better that Absolon wasn't there.

Better for Absolon.

He returned to the tailor in a foul mood made worse by a gloomy day, but the fine clothes improved it. The tailor spouted excuses for any defects and begged to be allowed more time to put them to rights, but Ragnar cut him off. He would return once he had everything he wished for and paid the tailor double his fee, which earned him effusive thanks. Ragnar left in disgust, despite the beautiful cut to the clothes that made him look every bit the noble.

He strutted down the street towards the castle, walking as if he owned the earth beneath his feet and the sky above his head. He stopped at the gate and at soldiers he didn't recognize. At the door he was permitted into the entry hall by a butler he didn't know, yet when asked who was being presented, the butler's eyebrows flicked up at his name.

"I wish to speak to my father."

The butler begged him wait and scurried off.

The great house echoed much as it had throughout his

life, emptied of the love of a mother or a father. Ragnar circled the great hall, spying the paintings that had hung there through much of his adolescence, at the family portraits and the battles extolling Sweden's victories on sea and land. He'd sat studying the painting of the Battle of Wallhof and saw himself in it, charging out of this hulk of cold stone and into glory for his country and for his family. But his father had always belittled him for those dreams.

The butler returned. "Sir, follow me."

How many of the staff would he keep? He'd lose all of them if he could. Couldn't have them becoming suspicious that he was more than a mortal man. He grimaced at the confines he would have to place on himself once more, watching what he said, what he did. Heroes should not be so constrained. He made a promise not to be so. It was being in this house, trapped within its walls full of rules and expectations that sought to bind him. He would not let it. It was just a house.

The butler led him into the drawing room, announced him, and left. But instead of his father, Ragnar was met by his brother, Peder, who stopped his pacing to watch him with trepidation and fear. He didn't move in for a brotherly hug, and Ragnar kept his distance.

Peder had changed little from the gruff, tall, thin man he'd been when Ragnar left to join the military all those years ago. Five years had passed since he'd seen him, having kept well away from the affairs of Jönköping so he could make his own fortune because he'd been given none to work with.

"Where's Father?"

Peder cleared his throat and straightened to his full height. "We thought you were dead."

"I've been hearing that a lot. Where is he?"

"He passed away. Around Christmastime."

His throat constricted. Almost a year. Knowing the bastard was dead carried none of the sweetness of being able to suck that shriveled soul out of his reptilian body. He'd missed his chance. He cracked his neck as rage bubbled up inside him. "Why wasn't I informed?"

"Would you have cared? We haven't heard from you in over a year."

"I was his son," he said through barely parted teeth. "Of course I would have cared." He would have been there to ensure his departure.

"I am surprised to hear that considering how little thought you gave him over the years. Foolishly we expected some word from you after your dismissal, but you stayed away. Father thought your shame must have been too great. I think he was relieved."

He narrowed his eyes and stalked towards Peder. "It's because of him I was expelled from the military."

"You led those five hundred men to their slaughter, not Father. The fault is entirely yours."

"What would you know of battle?" He brushed aside Peder's judgement, but he couldn't dispel the pricking at the back of his neck. "You sat in this castle far from strife and grew fat on his blind generosity, while I was out there earning glory for his name."

Peder scoffed and closed the gap between them to poke his bony, accusing finger into Ragnar's chest. "Soiling his name, you mean. You ran away to follow your little fantasies, and I stayed here, working for him and my family. I may be first born, but I built my position and proved to him that I was worthy of continuing his line. What are you but a failure?"

Ragnar popped his knuckles. The symbol blazed in the front of his mind like a flaming sword, and he would rip Peder's soul from him only after he'd tortured the bastard to within an inch of his sanity. He readied his hand to find the naked flesh of his throat. Everything would soon be as it should be with him ruling as head of the family for an eternity.

The door opened and in ran a little girl of no more than four years of age, calling out excitedly for her father. His wife, Kristina, followed behind. She blenched at recognizing him.

Peder scooped up the little girl into his arms, while Kristina hurried to her husband's side, never once taking her eyes off Ragnar. She sensed the danger they were in even if Peder's arrogance blinded him to it.

"You remember my brother, Ragnar?" Peder's happiness shone on his face as he looked upon his child, forgetting about Ragnar as if he was a servant.

"Of course," she said softly, her hand on her daughter, Peder's body partially shielding her. "You look well, brother."

He sneered.

"It's good to have you home. I know Peder has often wondered how you fared."

"Not enough to come searching."

"You're wrong," Peder said. "I did enquire after father died, foolishly thinking you should know of his death despite his feelings about you, but you had vanished. I had heard rumors you had become an outlaw, which didn't surprise me, but I could not track you down." He sighed. "Brother, I really did try to find you, but I figured if you were still alive, then you did not want to be found. And it seems you have done all right for yourself, if the fine clothes you are wearing are anything to go by."

He looked down at the fine jacket, at the costume he'd draped over his body in the hope he could finally take his rightful place in this family. If he could bring them glory, then maybe they could love him. But the clothes were a lie.

The only truth was that he didn't belong in that house. And not because he would never receive the love that he craved, but because it was all spoken for.

When he looked at his brother and his little family, he recognized those shared looks of affection and gentle touches. He had never had that.

Not until Absolon.

The berserker had tried to show him what was there the whole time. He'd even given him the power to achieve all he said he ever wanted. But Absolon's taunt spoke more truth that he would have wished.

He was Ragnar the Heartless, and he had no one to blame but himself.

The realization cleaved him in two.

What had he achieved in chasing old vengeance? It had brought neither him nor Absolon peace. He had run away from the chance for a love that was truly and freely given, despite all the terrible things he'd done, despite the bad treatment and the cursing and the railing against his lot. How had Absolon put up with him? And what had he shown in return except contempt? The anger drained out of him and the need to feed faded.

"Ragnar? Are you all right?" Peder asked.

"I am." Or at least he would be once he got back to Absolon. "I have to go."

"But you just arrived."

Kristina stepped forward. "Are you sure you won't stay?" Her hand trembled.

Peder showed no encouragement for her words, only confusion at his change of heart. But Ragnar was done with them. They were no longer his family nor his concern. One day they would die, but not by his hand. And he was at peace with that.

"Quite sure. I can see there is nothing for me here. I won't bother you again."

No one stopped him leaving, and once outside, he retrieved his peasant clothes and set course for Absolon. He only hoped he could find his way back.

$$\text{❧}\quad 9 \quad \text{☙}$$

Ragnar pushed himself hard in his rush to return to Absolon. The land passed in a blur and with the moon hiding her face, he could run on the open road. He retraced his journey, fearful at every moment that he might go the wrong way. He had no name for the village near Absolon's farm so couldn't ask a peasant or soldier for directions. All he could trust was that he had remembered the route.

He took over two days to reach the farm, stopping at the boundary where the forest gave way to the field. The ground had turned sodden and muddy from rain, and frost clung to the dirt. The red farmstead had none of the grandeur of the castle he'd come from, nor the riches he'd left behind as if they were nothing but scraps. But it contained Absolon, and that's all that mattered.

This was where Absolon wanted to be. This was the quiet life that Absolon wanted to have. Here he could lose himself in the fantasy of a working farm filled with animals, a field that grew, was harvested, lay fallow, and grew again. It could give their lives some rhythm beyond the eternal endlessness that was now their lot.

Because they weren't like mortal men.

And what could mortal men do that they could not overcome?

He crossed the field. On the journey he'd thought a lot about what he would say to win Absolon back. He'd apologize and beg for his forgiveness. He'd tell him he was wrong to leave, that he was weak, and that Absolon had given him so much—both immortality and his heart—that he would be forever grateful. His blood tickled with the thrill of seeing him again, of finally being where he should always have been—by Absolon's side. As he neared the door, he called out Absolon's name.

It opened and Absolon filled the frame.

Ragnar's heart lifted, raising his lips into a smile.

But there was no such happiness on Absolon's face. "What do you want?" The flatness in his voice had a sharp edge.

This was not going to be as easy as he expected.

He sank down onto his knees and clasped his hands together to plead. "I've come back to you. I've realized how wrong I was to leave you behind. I ran away. I was scared. But I now know how much you love me and how much you were trying to help me. I'm sorry for leaving like I did. Will you forgive me?"

"No."

Ragnar blinked. No? "What do you mean?" He'd come back. He'd apologized. He'd done the right thing. What more did Absolon want?

"I mean, no. Fuck off and leave me in peace." Absolon retreated into the house and prepared to slam the door.

It couldn't end like this.

Ragnar surged to his feet and blocked the door from closing. "Sol, please. I came back for you."

"I've heard enough of your lies to last me until my final days and soon I'll be free of them forever. You could at least have the decency to give me freedom until then."

"Final days? Sol, what do you mean?"

Absolon gave the door one final push but it wasn't enough to expel Ragnar from the house. He let go and turned away in disgust. "I'm ending it. I have eight days left then I'm going to my death."

Absolon's words winded him. He couldn't mean it, could he? "No, Sol, please, you can't do this." He staggered towards him. "Not because of me."

Absolon sneered. "You think I do this because of you? I do this for me. My whole life people have taken advantage of me for their own gain. My mother did it, my brothers and sisters, the generals, Lysander, and of course you." He jabbed at the air with his finger. "You took more from me than anyone has ever taken. You took my love, you destroyed my spirit, and you stole my soul."

"I know. I'm sorry. I didn't—"

Fire flashed in Absolon's eyes. "You didn't care. That was the problem. You didn't care what you took; you just took it, because you thought it was your right. And then you manipulated me into turning you into what I am. You made me believe that you wanted it so you could be with me and we would finally be equals."

Absolon dragged his fingers through his hair and his fists tightened in his locks. "And in my stupidity and my weakness, I relented. You know, I actually thought you would run away if I turned you. I spent two days arguing with myself about it, but like a fool I believed you were capable of love. That you wouldn't do that to me. So I gave you what I promised I'd never curse another human being with, and what did you do? You left." He waved his hand through the air as capriciously as Ragnar had been in his flight. "You barely stayed a day. Well, I'm sick of being used, and sick of contemplating an eternity with you haunting me. You can have it all. Have the glory that you so crave. Hell, you can even have the farm once I'm gone. And you can have a life free of anyone loving you ever again." Absolon towered over him and the hate carved his face into a death mask. "Now fuck off and let me have my wish. You can at least give me that."

He brushed past him, but Ragnar grabbed his arm and spun him round.

"Absolon, please, I'm sorry I did all that to you. I know how much hurt I have caused you, how I have wronged you, but please, you cannot do this. You cannot give yourself over to death when you have been given this gift."

"It's not a gift, it's a curse!"

"You're wrong, Sol." He sank to his knees. He would beg plead on broken glass if it showed the depth of his penance. But all he could use was his words. "It's a gift, because I have an eternity with you. I have been back through my old life and I have seen how wrong I was. Revenge left me hollow and I understand now it wasn't what I'd been craving. I was blind to the love you gave me because it frightened me. I was afraid I wouldn't be worthy of anyone's love, least of all yours."

Absolon's hand hung limp in his grasp. Acid dripped through Ragnar's veins. If he didn't fight for Absolon, he would be bound for a barren eternity.

"I didn't want to admit that love was already there for me if I wanted it. I thought it could be taken from me so easily, that it made me weak, that someone would hurt you and I would be broken utterly. I never understood that it was I who hurt you and in so doing hurt myself." He took up both hands. "Please, Absolon, I know I have done you much wrong. I stole your life from you, and I broke your heart more times that I should be forgiven for, but please, I have changed. I have seen that the life I could have with you is worth more than all the gold and praise and sagas put together."

The hard glint in Absolon's eyes did not soften. "You are a liar and you will always be one. Now get out of my house." He pulled himself free of Ragnar's grip and held the door open. He refused to meet Ragnar's gaze.

Was this it? Was there truly nothing he could say to make Absolon understand the depth of his love? He could feel it, running all the way through him, but how could he show it to Absolon? If he died, there would be no life left for him.

He stumbled to his feet and shuffled towards the door. He stopped in front of Absolon. "Please, Sol. There must be something I can do to keep you alive."

He lowered his face towards Ragnar like a snarling hound. "I would have my freedom from the pain of love. Now go ruin someone else's life." He shoved Ragnar out of the house and slammed the door.

He turned to knock. He would plead with Absolon again, if not to take him back then at least to reconsider his suicide. He pressed his hand against the wooden door. But what words could he say that he hadn't already? Absolon didn't trust any of them. And whose fault was that? He took a step back and traipsed across the field in a daze.

Eight days.

He had eight days before Absolon perished in which to find a reason for him to stay alive. Why couldn't it be him?

He knew why.

And he wished it wasn't so.

He slipped into the forest and walked with his head

down. Words no longer meant anything to Absolon, and perhaps they never had. They hadn't spoken much when they'd been holed up in the forest that first winter, yet he'd felt Absolon's love then as they eked out their living. He had to do something to show—

Pawprints tracked through the mud.

The dog…

He crouched and felt around them. They were fresh and led off to his left. He stared in their direction. He could get the dog back. If Absolon wouldn't live for him, then maybe he'd live for the dog. Despite what Absolon said, he was made to love, and it didn't have to be human.

He followed the tracks as far as he could, wending deeper into the forest, crossing and recrossing the stream. They disappeared at times and he had to expand his search to find where they picked up again, but towards the end of daylight he spied the dog in the distance.

He breathed out in relief. Now all he had to do was catch it. Trogen hadn't yet spotted him so he crept closer, keeping as quiet as possible, until he was within a *stenkast* of the reclining animal. He lowered himself into a sprinter's stance, digging his heel into the dirt to get plenty of power, then launched. He charged through the forest towards the dog and swept it into his arms before it knew what had happened.

He'd done it! He'd caught the dog!

But his elation was short-lived as the dog fought and snarled and sank its teeth into his arm. He dropped it out of fear, and the dog fled. Ragnar cursed its retreating backside, but when his frustration subsided and he was left alone in twilight, he knew the blame was all his. Of course it wouldn't be that easy, and now he'd wasted one of Absolon's few remaining precious days. There was no point in chasing the dog now. The more he stormed through the forest, the more likely it was that the dog would keep running.

He sank to the ground and rested against a tree trunk. He'd have to bide his time until the morning came and try again. Trogen had given his trust easily when they'd first met in his cell, which is how he'd been able to use him against Absolon, but regaining it would require time Absolon may not have.

The next day Ragnar stayed in the area, the many tracks in the ground a sign that Trogen preferred it. He hunted, caught a hare and a pheasant, and built a fire over which to roast them in the hope the smell would draw the dog near.

But he stayed away.

Ragnar scattered the cooked meat in a broad radius around his camp and waited, anxiety over the passing hours urging him to do more, or at least to go see Absolon. But he refrained. He sat and dug his hands into the soil as if they were roots taking hold. He didn't see Trogen the entire day, but he remained through that day and the next with no reward.

The following day he hunted again and set the kills to cooking, while checking what had been taken and what left. In place of meat, he found pawprints and breathed out a heavy sigh. It was a start. There were only five days left, but he knew he was on the right path. He laid out more meat and waited, and in the late afternoon was rewarded with the sight of Trogen standing on a rocky ledge looking down on him. He remained for a second then turned tail and ran. But it didn't dishearten him. He would try again.

With four days remaining, he didn't scatter the meat as far and laid trails leading to Ragnar's position. Absolon's nearing demise constricted Ragnar's throat, but he continued on. He couldn't hurry the dog, and Absolon would not listen to his words. He had to be patient, even knowing how close to the end he was getting.

Ragnar waited by the campfire, the smell of charred meat wafting through the air. He held onto a pheasant's leg while another rabbit cooked over the fire. Trogen had to come. Absolon couldn't die.

The sound of crunching bones and contented growls came from behind Ragnar's back. He turned slowly to see the russet hound munching on its meal, happy in its gluttony. When Ragnar rotated in his place, the dog looked up and cocked its head, its tongue lolling out of its mouth. Its ears were up. Ragnar allowed himself a smile.

He held out the pheasant leg and called softly to the dog. A tense minute passed before Trogen stood, sniffed the air, and approached. Ragnar stayed where he was, careful not to spook the animal, but he worried his heart was thundering loud enough to scare him away. Trogen reached forward with his snout, wary of getting too close yet still eager for a feed. Ragnar held it out further, and Trogen took it in his jaw and sank to the spot to eat.

He breathed again, fully aware of how much stock he was putting into this endeavor. He wanted to go to it and scratch behind its ears or coax it into his arms, but he wasn't yet certain of the animal's trust.

When Trogen finished, he stood and ambled closer, snuffling under Ragnar's hand to lick the meat juices from his skin. The rough and eager tongue made him laugh but he kept his voice quiet, changing from a chuckle into a hum, to sing to the dog as it lay in the dirt and rested its head in Ragnar's lap. He sang as he stroked the thick wiry hair on the dog's back. Trogen climbed into Ragnar's lap, curled up in the warmth that Ragnar provided, and fell asleep. Ragnar sang all afternoon, his hand on Trogen's back, and his heart quiet and at peace.

Tomorrow, he would save Absolon.

When morning came and Ragnar woke, Trogen was not in his lap. He called softly, hoping the dog at least knew the sound of his voice, if not his name. Had Trogen abandoned him? He searched, trying to keep the frantic tone out of his voice. As he neared the rock ledge, Trogen appeared at the top, letting out a cheerful bark.

Ragnar relaxed. "How about we go for a walk?" He set off towards the farm, slapping his thigh to bring Trogen to his side. The dog bounded over, allowed a scratch behind his ears, and gamboled ahead, chasing birds from their hollows and scent-marking as he went.

Absolon had three days left. What if this didn't work? What if Trogen was not enough to keep Absolon alive? He paused at the edge of the field with the dog by his side, his tail wagging as he looked up at him. "I guess this is it, Trogen."

No matter what happened, he needed to try.

He marched across the field. It seemed to take an age to reach the house and yet the journey was over too soon. Sweat slicked his palms, and he wiped them on his coat, his fist hesitating as it hovered in front of Absolon's door. Trogen sat beside him, looking expectantly. Perhaps he thought he was going to be fed. At least he expected something; Ragnar didn't know what he wanted to happen.

He understood though, as long as it had taken to gain, that whatever Absolon decided was his choice. He hoped it was the one that would keep him in the world. He flexed his shoulders, took a deep breath, and knocked.

Absolon opened the door. Ragnar opened his mouth to speak. Until that moment he had hoped Absolon would be so grateful he'd brought the dog back that he'd take him back too. But seeing the sorrow and despair in Absolon's eyes and knowing he was the cause of so much of it, what he wanted didn't matter as long as Absolon lived.

Ragnar looked down at Trogen and pointed into the house. "Go!"

Trogen stood and hurried inside, a quick sniff and friendly yip for Absolon as he passed.

"What is this?"

"If you won't stay alive for me, at least stay alive for Trogen." He wanted to say more but his words never meant much. He wanted to touch Absolon's cheek, or rest a hand over his heart, but his touch was more poisoned than ever. He turned and ran before he changed his mind.

❧ 10 ❧

Snow lay thick upon the forest floor, the stark and bare trees speared the sky, and all around was still, silent, dead. Ragnar stood at the door to the little stone building that was now his home and stared across the desolation. This was his lot.

It was where he had lived with Absolon after his dismissal, and then, to his shame, used as a stronghold for his loot. Since returning three months earlier, he'd raided its coffers to pay for comforts they couldn't afford in the beginning and ones he later didn't need—a bed, a padded chair, candles and books. He repaired the roof so it wouldn't leak and installed a hearth and a chimney so he could warm his home.

His home…

In three months, that's what he'd made. A home. Far from Absolon. Far from anyone but for the unlucky who wandered too close to his dwelling. He understood the Skogsrå then.

When it came time to harvest and no soul showed up at his door, he entered a village beyond the forest's boundaries and delivered a merciful death to sustain himself. After a harvest, he returned to the forest, tipped out the stones from one jar into another, and began his count again. It was a life.

And so Ragnar the Red's days passed.

He was too scared to venture much farther, afraid that he'd find himself at Absolon's farm and find him gone. He wanted no confirmation that Absolon had died and so could continue to believe that he lived. He allowed himself that one delusion now that he'd cast away all others.

He was not a hero.

He did not deserve love simply because he demanded it.

He mattered no more than any other man.

So, he lived alone where he could do little harm. He chopped wood. He walked the forest. As an indulgence, he bought books and read them over and over to pass the time.

Not that it appeared to be passing much at that moment. He turned back into his house, closed the door, and settled into his chair. He picked up a book, eager to lose himself in some distraction, when a dog's muffled bark broke the quiet.

He stopped. A dog would mean a hunter. He sighed and bowed his head. He could let him go; he had not yet stumbled up to his door and may yet pass by without notice, but the smoke twisting out of the chimney would give him away and draw the stranger near.

The dog's excited barks grew louder. Whatever hunter this was, his hound was undisciplined. He'd have scared off any prey by now, but there was joy in the dog's heralding, and it made him think of Trogen.

Which made him think of Absolon.

He grimaced. Whoever the hunter was, he would leave

the forest safely. Ragnar had no desire to break them apart, not even to protect his tiny castle.

The barks came closer, taking on a more immediate sound. Perhaps he could welcome them after all. He had no food or drink, but he had a warm hearth and a bed to sleep in. He could be as generous as possible, and if the hunter was poor, he could load him with treasure.

He was getting carried away, but his self-imposed isolation had made him sentimental and more eager for the company of others than he would have expected. He put the book back on the table. He would find the hunter. He went to the door, turned the handle, and opened it.

He only had a second to take in Absolon standing there —a second for his heart to rise on a draught of warm air flecked with snow, a second for his blood to sparkle— before Absolon barged in, scooped Ragnar into his arms, and pressed him against the door frame. Their lips met, and Absolon's mouth moved against his as strongly as his body pressed against Ragnar's.

This was real. It had to be. None of his dreams had held such strength. Those lips felt like Absolon's lips. Those arms felt like Absolon's arms. That love felt like Absolon's love. Or it would if Ragnar hadn't burned it out of him. He pushed Absolon away, ripping out his heart by the roots.

"Wait, Sol, what is this? Why are you here?"

It truly was Absolon, dressed in a thick fur-lined coat and a woolen hat, and with Trogen—yes, Trogen!— sniffing at his boots. This was not some magic that the forest had conjured, merely a miracle. And one he didn't deserve.

He went inside the house and sat on the edge of his bed. He didn't want to invite Absolon in only for him to leave again, but he followed anyway, taking up the chair opposite. Trogen sat at Ragnar's feet and put a paw on his leg. He didn't have any food for the dog, but he gave him a scratch which pleased him.

"I had to find you."

"But why? You're better off without me, even I know that."

Absolon laughed air through his nose. "For a while there, I agreed with you. I was even going to end it all, even after you brought the dog back, just to spite you."

Ragnar's heart wept quicksilver.

"But with one day left, I decided I didn't want to die and leave Trogen behind. He was a good companion, and so I harvested and lived. I would have stayed there, but every time I looked at the dog, I thought of you and what you had done for me."

"It was the least I could do after the trouble I've brought you in your life."

Absolon pulled the woolen hat off his head and twisted it in his hands. "It's more than most have ever done." He leaned back into the chair, and Ragnar liked the look of him there, not easy as such, not quite comfortable, but close and in his home where he could take in this view of him and ease his heart of its worrying over whether Absolon lived.

All before he left again.

"Then you should have taken that small amount and kept it. Why come here?"

He shrugged half-heartedly. "The farm got lonely. It felt empty. All of it—my house, the store, the stables, the fields. They were as empty as I felt because you had gone."

"It was better I did."

"Yes, it was. Then." Absolon cleared his throat. "But I realized that you had changed. When you brought Trogen back you did that for me alone, and I thought…I hoped…

it would mean we could be different than we were. So that's why I had to find you."

Absolon told him of his journey, of the decimation he found at the garrison, but also what he'd found in Jönköping.

"You left your family untouched. I spoke to them because I wanted to know for sure you'd been there. They were worried about you and said that you hadn't seemed stable, but seeing that you'd left them alive, I said they had nothing to worry about."

That was true; he had no desire to go back there.

Absolon got off the chair and sat next to him on the bed. "I knew then, that even after I had rejected you, even after you had brought Trogen back to me, that you were different from the person you had been. You were better. You were enough and no longer striving to be someone else."

Ragnar turned his head to look into Absolon's imploring gaze. "And what now?"

"Now I know you are worthy of my love, and I hope I am worthy of yours. And, if you'll have me, there is no one I would rather spend eternity with."

Could he believe it? Could he trust it? Did he want it?

The answer to all three was a resounding yes.

He placed his hand against Absolon's cheek, drawn to the bewitching hope of his gaze and the expectant grin on his lips, and kissed Absolon. The anticipation broke him apart and he breathed everything he ever was and could ever be into that connection. He surrendered the last piece of himself to Absolon's love and with the ruin of his defenses bestowed upon Absolon everything he had to give. The fervor of his kisses, the blaze of his love, and the passion of his soul joined with Absolon's to create one perfect union. They were complete and nothing in the world could tear them apart again.

Absolon shivered as he broke the kiss. Pleasure rippled through Ragnar's body, bursting with the full realization of everything that love between them could be. He smiled up at Absolon, his lips buzzing with need.

"Is that a yes?"

He laughed. "Yes, yes, a thousand years of yes."

Absolon grabbed him and pulled him back onto the bed. They tore their clothes from each other and filled the stone house with the sounds of their ecstasy. When they were done, and curled in each other's arms, Ragnar felt as at peace as the winter that lay beyond their door. It was a peace not of death, but of promise for what lay ahead and what they would witness and endure together.

Forever.

ABOUT THE AUTHOR

Daniel de Lorne writes about men, monsters and magic.

In love with writing since he wrote a story about a talking tree at age six, his first novel, the romantic horror *Beckoning Blood*, was published in 2014. At the heart of every book is a romance between two men, whether they're irresistible vampires, historical hotties, or professional paramours.

In his other life, Daniel is a professional writer and researcher in Perth, Australia, with a love of history and nature. All of which makes for great story fodder.

And when he's not working, he and his husband explore as much of this amazing world as they can, from the ruins of Welsh abbeys to trekking famous routes and swimming with whales.

Connect with Daniel and get a FREE short story. Be the first to know about new releases, cover reveals, giveaways and more.
www.danieldelorne.com